PETER CORRIS is known as the 'godfather' of Australian crime fiction through his Cliff Hardy detective stories. He has written in many other areas, including a co-authored autobiography of the late Professor Fred Hollows, a history of boxing in Australia, spy novels, historical novels and a collection of short stories about golf (see www.petercorris. net). In 2009, Peter Corris was awarded the Ned Kelly Award for Best Fiction by the Crime Writers Association of Australia. He is married to writer Jean Bedford and has lived in Sydney for most of his life. They have three daughters and six grandsons.

The Cliff Hardy collection

PETER CORRIS
AFTERSHOCK

ALLEN&UNWIN
SYDNEY • MELBOURNE • AUCKLAND • LONDON

This edition published by Allen & Unwin in 2014
First published by Bantam Books, a division of Transworld Publishers, in 1991

Allen & Unwin
83 Alexander Street
Crows Nest NSW 2065
Australia
Phone: (61 2) 8425 0100
Email: info@allenandunwin.com
Web: www.allenandunwin.com

Cataloguing-in-Publication details are available
from the National Library of Australia
www.trove.nla.gov.au

ISBN 978 1 76011 014 7 (pbk)
ISBN 978 1 74343 796 4 (ebook)

Printed and bound in Australia by Griffin Press

MIX
Paper from
responsible sources
FSC® C009448
www.fsc.org

The paper in this book is FSC certified.
FSC promotes environmentally responsible,
socially beneficial and economically viable
management of the world's forests.

For Jean, again

1

Horrie Jacobs was one of the smallest adults ever to walk into my office. With his shoes on his feet and his hat on his head he still wouldn't have topped five feet by more than an inch. He was a compactly built, neat old man in a grey suit, no tie and with the *Newcastle Herald* under his arm. He made the office look big, which it isn't.

'My name's Horrie Jacobs, Mr Hardy. I'm from Newcastle.'

I shook his hand and waved him into the client's chair, thinking that Novocastrians do that. You don't find Wollongongites saying 'I'm from Wollongong'. I have a feeling they might do it a bit in Queensland—'I'm from Rocky'— that kind of thing. I sat behind my desk, which is from Darlinghurst Office Disposals, and asked Mr Jacobs what I could do for him.

He sat, put his newspaper on the floor by his chair, took off his hat and said, 'You've heard of the Newcastle earthquake?'

I nodded. Who hadn't? It rocked Sydney and parts south, east and west, caused a lot of

1

damage in Newcastle and killed about a dozen people up there.

'I lived in Newcastle all my life, never saw anything like it.' Horrie Jacobs fiddled with his hat. 'Bricks flying around in the air. I missed out on the war but I reckon it must've been something like that. One of them bricks hit you and you were a goner.'

I'd taken out a notepad and written down the date and the client's name the way the regulations governing the private enquiry agent's trade say to do, but I wasn't too hopeful of getting any business here. I judged his age to be about seventy. He looked like a man who'd worked hard all his life. His skin was weatherbeaten and his hands had the enlargement that goes with manual work. You don't see it much anymore; I couldn't remember ever having a client with wrists and hands like Horrie's—not a paying client. And natural disasters bring them out of the woodwork—compensation nuts, litigation freaks.

I doodled on the pad—120, 150, 175—the sliding scale of per diem dollar rate I daydreamed about charging clients according to their problems and means. The trouble was, I hadn't had any clients since I'd come up with the idea. If the Treasurer wanted the economy to slow I could show him what snail's pace was, right here. I decided to be kind. 'I don't handle insurance matters, Mr Jacobs. I don't know if you've dealt with any of the big insurance companies lately, but they're not too unreasonable and you can get legal help with . . . '

Jacobs leaned forward in the uncomfortable chair. 'I don't need legal help, mate. I'm not after insurance. I live at Dudley, fifteen miles out of Newcastle. I felt the bloody quake but I didn't lose anything. Not so much as a bloody glass.'

'Good,' I said. 'Well, what's the problem?' As he leaned forward I noticed that his suit was well cut and that his pale blue shirt was medium expensive. I cursed the Treasurer and circled 150 on the pad.

He looked around the room, taking in the basic furnishings and low level of maintenance. I'd never heard of Dudley. Maybe it was a place for rich, retired jockeys and horse trainers or film stunt men. With his looks and build Horrie could have been any of these. In any case he seemed to be used to a better standard of accommodation. 'What do you charge?' he said.

I improvised. 'A hundred and twenty a day, plus expenses. Seven day retainer, fifty per cent returnable if nothing works out after three days. I have to tell you that private enquiry agents' fees are seldom tax deductable.'

'I don't have to worry about tax,' Horrie said. 'You stack the odds a bit your way, eh?'

'How's that?' I said.

'You get three and a half days' pay guaranteed out of seven. By rights, it should be three. Not that it matters a bugger to me. I can afford it.'

I was starting to appreciate Mr Jacobs. I like Newcastle and if his business took me there so much the better. Good for the expense sheet and with summer coming on it'd be good to get out of Sydney. I saw myself surfing at Stockton Beach while earning 120 dollars a day for . . . doing what? Surely nothing risky or dirty, not for a nice old guy like Horrie? His suit wasn't *that* good. 'Better give me your full name and address, Mr Jacobs, also your occupation.'

Horrie tossed his hat on to the desk, took out a packet of Senior Service and slid it open. 'You mind? Got to say that these days.'

'Go ahead,' I said, and just stopped myself commenting that at his age what would be the harm. I pushed the glass ashtray that had had nothing in it but dust for a few weeks towards him and got ready to write and fight the tobacco craving. I stopped years ago, but it never goes away.

Horrie lit up with a disposable lighter, puffed luxuriously and flicked ash expertly into the glass jigger. A smoker's smoker.

'Horace Reginald Jacobs, sixty-nine, 7 Bombala Street, Dudley. Retired miner. Married forty years, four kids, fourteen grandchildren.'

'Congratulations,' I said.

He puffed angrily. 'That supposed to be smart?'

'No, I meant it. Especially about being married that long. That's getting rare these days. About the kids, I wouldn't know. I've never had any.'

He stubbed out the less than half-smoked cigarette and took a good look at me. His pale blue eyes were surrounded by wrinkles and his face had started to cave in but not into those disapproving lines you often see. Horrie had the look of a man more interested in life than critical of it. He was looking at a face well past forty with a broken nose and a few scars from fists and bad habits. Like him I had a full head of hair but whereas his was white with a bit of dark still in it mine was the reverse. 'You're no spring chicken but it wouldn't be too late to start.'

I smiled and shook my head. In one marriage and three or four serious relationships the subject had never come up. That had to mean something. 'Perhaps you can tell me why you're here, Mr Jacobs.'

'Don't you want to know how I can afford to pay you?'

I shrugged. 'Your suit says you can. My guess is you got a good redundancy package. Good luck to you.'

He snorted. 'You'd be wrong. I worked till the day I turned sixty-five. I got a decent super but nothing special. No, mate, the reason I can sit here with my cheque book in the pocket of a tailored suit and listen to you talk about a hundred and twenty bucks a day is that I won the Lotto a couple of weeks after I retired. Over a million.'

'That's terrific,' I said. 'You look to be in good health, your family sounds OK. I can't see that you should have a problem in the world.'

'I wouldn't, if the bloody coppers and other pen pushers'd do their jobs. But they just reckon I'm old and rich and crazy and tell me to piss off.'

We were getting to it now. Some kind of bureaucratic bungle to do with the earthquake. Horrie was a miner. Maybe he knew there was a shaft under the Workers' Club that had collapsed and killed ten or so pensioners. That'd be interesting but a bit out of my line. Ombudsman territory.

I must have looked dubious because Horrie's voice took on a pleading note. 'I need your help, Mr Hardy. I was put onto you by someone from the radio in Kempsey.'

I was getting ready to doodle again but what he said made me grip the pencil so hard I almost snapped it. 'Who?'

'Woman named Helen Broadway. See, I got desperate when no-one in Newcastle'd listen to me and I started ringing the radio stations trying to get on air. Well, I got nowhere. But this Broadway woman gave me the time of day. She said she couldn't put me on the air but she advised me to get in touch with you. I told her that I wasn't short of a bob, see?'

Helen Broadway. I hadn't seen her for three years but sometimes I dreamed that we were still together and laughing at something, walking somewhere, making love in one of the many ways. I never knew whether to call these good dreams or bad. They left me feeling thinned out and desperate. The antidote was to think of our last fight, over commitment and priorities and how hopeless it had all been. It was a jolt to hear her name being spoken by a stranger. I wrote 'referred by H. Broadway' in block capitals on the pad and tried to switch

6

the past off and tune in to the present. 'Tell me what you told her, Mr Jacobs.'

As a story-teller, Horrie Jacobs was a good miner. He started well back from the work-face with an account of how he met his mate, Oscar Bach. 'He was a funny bloke, Oscar. I met him on Dudley beach, fishing. I'm a keen beach fisherman, see? Oscar was a new chum but he got the hang of it pretty quick. We caught some bloody huge bream and flathead, me and Oscar. He was a bit impatient, wouldn't look for the gutter properly. Couldn't wait to get his line in. I showed him a few things. He loved catching fish.'

I felt I had to steer things a little. 'Was he a miner, too?'

'Oscar? No fear. I tried to take him down the pit once, just to show him how it was. He stepped into the cage and stepped straight out again. Couldn't face it. No, Oscar had his own business. He was in the pest control game. You know, spraying and laying down poison for cockroaches and that. He was in it in a small way, but he did all right. Just rented a cottage in Dudley, nothing flash. He didn't like the work much, especially getting under houses, but he was his own boss and he liked that.'

Horrie Jacobs lit another cigarette and gazed in the direction of my single window. As it happened, he was looking north and that was where his thoughts were. 'We were good mates, me and Oscar, for going on five years. I'd been a bit short of friends ever since I gave up the grog. Miners, you know, they all drink like crazy. When you stop, you lose your mates.'

I nodded. I could easily imagine it happening. One of the reasons I've never stopped.

'I had to stop. I was getting a belly, couldn't work properly. The wife hated it. So, I stopped. Oscar didn't touch it. Never had. Said he didn't like the taste. He was a bit of a fitness fanatic, too. Walked everywhere. I don't suppose you know Dudley?'

'No. What's it near?'

'Redhead.'

'I've surfed there. Years ago.'

'Yeah, big surfing beach. Dudley's different. Couldn't even drive to it till a couple of years ago when they put a dirt road in. Still doesn't get a lot of use. It's all recreation reserve around there, the foreshore and that. You can stand on parts of Dudley beach and not see anything man-made. Anyway, I'd drive down to where the track starts and walk to the beach. Fifteen minutes down the track. Oscar'd walk from home every time. Put another fifteen minutes on the time to get there. And he'd always walk back, wouldn't accept a lift. Big bloke, very strong. Twenty years younger than me.'

I had a picture of the two men, old and middle-aged, tiny and large, the quintessential Australian and the man with the European name. Bach. What was that? What nationality was the composer? German? And Jacobs? Was that Jewish? Was the picture even more bizarre than I first thought? 'Are you having some sort of dispute with Mr Bach, Mr Jacobs?'

His eyebrows shot up and he almost choked

on the cigarette. 'Me and Oscar? Never. Best of mates. Never had a blue. Not once.' Course the wife didn't altogether take to him. She's a bit on the old-fashioned side, May. Oscar being a German was a bit of a trouble to her. She lost some family in the war.'

I could see that Horrie was going to tell the story in his own way at his own pace. I wrote May Jacobs on the pad and put German alongside Bach's name. Johann Sebastian. Of course, what else could he be. 'But that didn't worry you?'

Horrie butted the cigarette only half-smoked, as before. 'Me? No. I worked on the Snowy River scheme with blokes from all over the world—Germans, Poles, Yugoslavs, Czechs, you name it. Good blokes and bastards, same as us. Oscar was a good bloke.'

He reached into the breast pocket of his suit coat and took out a leather wallet. From the wallet he extracted a newspaper clipping. He unfolded it and pushed it across the desk to me. The clipping was from the *Newcastle Herald* of 3 July. It was a report on the opening of the inquest into the deaths caused by the Newcastle earthquake. The bulk of the report focussed on those killed within seconds of 10.27 a.m., when the quake hit, in the collapse of the Workers' Club in the city centre. Also under enquiry were the deaths of two men and a woman caused by falling glass and masonry in Hamilton and that of Oscar Bach, forty-eight, who had died when part of a church had fallen

9

on him Mr Bach had been treating the church's foundations for pest infestation at the time. The bit about Bach had been underlined.

I scanned the clipping quickly. It looked as if a lot of the blame was going to fall on the city fathers who'd put in unstable land fills in the Newcastle area. Safe target. I'd followed the inquest in a random way at the time and remembered these findings. I hadn't remembered the name of Oscar Bach. If I'd been running a modern, high-tech operation I'd have passed the clipping over to a secretary to run through the Nashua. Not here in St Peters Lane, Darlinghurst. I returned the clipping and was encouraged to see that Horrie had put a cheque book on the desk beside his wallet. 'That must have been a shock,' I said. 'To lose a friend like that.'

'That's the point, mate. I didn't lose him like that. I saw Oscar Bach alive and well at 10.32. That's five minutes *after* the bloody earthquake.'

2

I sat up straight in my chair and took a new look at Horrie Jacobs. An ex-miner with a weatherbeaten face. What did that mean? Nothing. He was a fisherman as well as a miner. What sort of a miner forms a friendship with a German pest controller? I brushed that one aside immediately. One of the few Australian historians I'd ever read was Manning Clark and his remark that 'life was immense' had always struck me as true. Friendships could be as various as anything else. Horrie Jacobs' old, pale eyes bored steadily into me. 'That's the problem, Mr Hardy. My mate Oscar didn't die in the earthquake. Someone killed him and put him down in all that busted up brick and mortar under the church. But no-one'll listen to me.'

'Let's tackle it from the official angle first,' I said. 'I'm not saying this is the right angle. Just that it's best to see how the system's dealt with it.'

'The system's shoved it under the bloody carpet,' Horrie muttered.

'What did the inquest find?'

11

He opened the wallet again and took out another clipping. He looked at it and shook his head. 'Death by misadventure. Want to see?'

'Not now. Did you give evidence, Mr Jacobs?'

'No. That's the snag. I rushed off to see that May was all right. Some silly bugger ran into me and I finished up in hospital with cuts and concussion. I was out of it for a few days. When I came around I was worried about May more than myself. But she was okay. I'm not as young as I used to be and I've got plenty of money. They cotton-woolled me for a while. It was a week or more before I heard that Oscar had been killed in the quake. I tried to tell them that was bullshit, but they wouldn't listen. Not even May believed me. They reckoned the car accident had scrambled my brains. Do I sound confused to you?'

I shook my head. 'No.'

'Bloody right I'm not. I saw Oscar in the street outside that church a couple of minutes after the whole bloody place had stopped shaking. What's more, he saw me.'

'He waved or something?'

'No, but I could tell he saw me. Then he moved towards the back of the church. That's when I took off for home.'

'The clipping says the church was in Hamilton.'

'That's right, Holy Cross in Beaumont Street. I own a little house near there, place May and me raised our family in. I rent it out to an old miner I worked with. Don't charge him much, just enough so's he can keep his pride, understand?' I nodded, I was beginning to like Horrie Jacobs more and more, and not just for his cheque book.

'Look, Mr Hardy, they've got it all stacked against me. I'm not young and my eyesight's not a hundred per cent. Also it was a bloody madhouse in the street, like I said. Glass flying, bricks ... I didn't stand there with a pair of binoculars trained on Oscar's face. But I saw him!'

Horrie wasn't the sort of man you'd call a fool or a liar. He obviously believed that what he was saying was true, which didn't mean it *was*, but meant it'd take some kind of proof to make him think otherwise. An investigation, in other words. I was convincing myself that there was a job here, but Horrie had bowled up one formidable obstacle.

'You say *they've* stacked the cards against you. Who's they?'

He seemed to be considering another cigarette. He rejected the idea and pushed the packet away. That was an interesting sign—refusing the props when the tough time came. 'You name 'em,' he said.

'What does your wife think?'

'She didn't like Oscar. That buggers up her judgement. She doesn't believe me. Thinks the concussion made me muddle up things that happened before the quake and after. I can't talk to her about it anymore. It upsets us too much. Ralph's even worse.'

'Ralph?'

'My son. Told you I had four kids—one son,

13

three daughters. Ralph's been more trouble than the three girls put together, but he's all right. Doesn't want to hear about me seeing Oscar, but.'

'You talked to the police?'

'Too right. Soon as I heard what they were saying about Oscar. They didn't want to know. You hear anything about the stink over the emergency services and so on?'

I tried to remember. 'There was some criticism—the ambulance men against the police, or the police against the fire brigade. I didn't really follow it. I remember the stuff about developers knocking down buildings that didn't need to go.'

Horrie nodded vigorously. 'That's another story. Don't get me started on that. Yeah, there were some balls-ups in the rescue job. Seems the cops went in a bit heavy-handed. It's hard to say. They probably did their best and it can't have been much bloody fun poking around in those buildings not knowing if a wall was going to fall on you. The whisper was the police knocked down a wall a bit early and might have made it harder to get some people out. I don't know. But anyway, the last thing they wanted was someone saying everything wasn't on the up and up as far as the dead were concerned. . .'

'I see. There was some looting, wasn't there?'

'Right. Would you believe it? Some bastard pinched a few cases of beer out of the club where people had lost their lives. Bloody terrible. My point is, the whole town got its wits back pretty quick and started to pull together—

committees, funds set up, relief centres, all that. I kicked in a few dollars myself. But no-one wanted to hear anything new or different. The whole thing was wrapped up, see?'

'Yes. What would you want me to do, Mr Jacobs?'

Horrie was agitated and suddenly looked his years. He took a cigarette now and lit it slowly, the way a tired person does. The first draw seemed to calm him. 'Mrs Broadway said she wasn't going to just drop it. Said she'd do some poking around, but she also told me how good you were at your job. She said you had a knack for talking to people and finding things out. I want you to find out about Oscar.'

'You were his friend,' I said. 'You must . . . '

He waved the cigarette dismissively. 'I knew bugger all about him. What I can tell you'd take two minutes. But I know this—someone killed him and shoved him into that rubble. Did it bloody quick and smooth, too. He must've had an enemy. I want to know who it was.'

I watched him as he puffed on his cigarette and resumed looking at my dirty window. I thought I knew what was going through his head. Sure, he wanted to know who had killed his friend as any normal person would. But there was more to it than that. An old, proud man had had his reliability, physical and mental, challenged and he wanted to meet the challenge. I judged that it had taken a lot of soul-searching for him to ask for my kind of help. I was in. I took the standard client form from the top drawer in the desk and scribbled in Horrie's details while he continued to smoke and look north. In the space for NATURE OF INVESTIGATION I wrote: 'O. Bach—circumstances of death of.' I slid the form across the desk and he signed it. He wrote me a cheque for eight hundred and forty dollars and I agreed to meet him in Beaumont Street, Hamilton tomorrow, at midday. He collected his paper from the floor, his hat from the desk and put away his wallet and cheque book. We shook hands and he left.

Down by the filing cabinet I had a case of Lindeman's claret a satisfied client had given me three months back. That is to say, I had what was left of the case—three bottles. I uncorked one of them and poured the wine into one of the number of mis-matched glasses I keep around the office. This was a pub middy glass and I half-filled it. I sipped the drink as I sat at my desk with the evidence of a job in front of me—a story, questions that needed answering, conflicts, a signature and a cheque. *Intriguing. Your lucky day, Cliff. And remember that you like Newcastle.* I drank some wine but I wasn't thinking about earthquakes and falling bricks, I was thinking about Helen Broadway.

It had been three years since the last angry words, the last door slamming and terse telephone conversation. Since then, nothing. As far as I knew she was still with her husband, the gentleman vintner, still a part-time producer at Radio Kempsey, still a mother. Now it sounded as if she'd made a switch and was on the air herself. I could see it—she was well-read, insatiably curious and had a knack of making

16

people feel good. I could imagine her getting some redneck National Party politician talking until he wished he hadn't. I wondered if she'd made any other changes. Knowing that she'd recommended me to Horrie Jacobs gave me the best feeling I'd had in a long time. It frightened me, too. The pain of our break-up was still with me. Like the Malayan War and my stint in Long Bay, it wasn't something I wanted to go through again. Then, I found myself thinking about the distance between Newcastle and Kempsey. Five hundred kilometres? Less?

I finished the wine and pushed the cork firmly into the bottle. I tidied up the few bits of paperwork I had lying about and took Horrie's cheque to the bank. His eight hundred and forty dollars didn't have much company in my operating account, but my credit cards were paid up and I'd met the mortgage for that month. The Falcon was newly registered and I hadn't been really drunk for a month. Things could've been worse. I strolled along Crown Street and down into Surry Hills to the office of the *Challenger*, an independent monthly started by Harry Tickener after he left the corporate clutches of the *News* organisation. Harry runs the tabloid with a skeleton staff from an office in Kippax Street, not far from where the big boys of the media game play. He'd recruited some of the best people he'd worked with in the palmy days of radical journalism and the *Challenger* looked fresh and exciting every month. So far. The paper was in its crucial second year, with a rising circulation, good

17

advertising support but battling against the economic tides like everything else.

I took the lift to the third floor and stuck my head inside the always open door. Everybody, that is the whole four of them, was on the phone. Harry beckoned me in and pointed me towards a stack of the latest issue of the broadsheet due out in a few days. The artwork was stark and dramatic—a map of Australia was being eaten away at the edges by some poisonous, corrosive substance. Cape York was half gone; the Great Australian Bight was gobbling the Nullarbor. The headline was THE DIRTY DOZEN—THE COMPANIES THAT ARE GIVING AUSTRALIA CANCER. I took a seat, nodded to the other workers and flicked through the paper. Harry's own passions were to the fore: conservation, freedom of the individual, social and political satire, readable books, drinkable wine.

He put the phone down and took a nicarette from a packet on his desk. Harry cold-turkeyed from sixty Camels a day when he started the *Challenger*. He reckoned one form of suicidal insanity was enough. He sucked unenthusiastically and pointed to the paper. 'What would you say?'

'Four bucks' worth,' I said. It cost five.

'Bastard,' Harry said. 'That's the best issue yet. I confidently expect six writs.'

'Can you afford that?'

Harry ran his hand over the thinning thatch of fair hair that always made him look like a country boy although he wasn't. 'We've got back-up. If we can get a couple of those fuckers into court we'll make them look very silly.'

'Good luck,' I said. 'I'll renew my subscription if you think you'll last.'

'Do it. And with the pleasantries over, what do you want, Cliff?'

'I want to look at the cuts on the Newcastle earthquake.'

Harry's laugh bounced off the far wall. Since he gave up smoking he's got a lot more wind to laugh with. 'What cuts? You think we can afford to clip papers and file them? Forget it. The cuts, mate, are over there.'

He was pointing at several metre-high stacks of newspapers on a bench running the length of a wall. I glanced around the room—Pauline, the secretary and organiser was hammering at a keyboard; Jack Singer, the sub-editor, was reading a stack of faint faxes by holding them up to the light; Beth Lewis, the lay-out person, was sticking captions under photographs on a proof sheet.

'No help there, Cliff,' Harry said. 'It's all do-it-yourself around this place. December 28 and on. What's the problem?'

'I'm interested in the inquest, too.'

'July and August. Go to it.'

I groaned and got out of my chair to walk over to the bench. I heard a rustle of broadsheet and turned to see Harry smiling at me and holding out several sheets of typescript.

'What's so funny?' I said. 'You look as if you've just won Editor of the Year.'

'All in good time. I just thought you'd want to have a look at this. It was submitted for the

Miscellany page which, being a devoted reader of the publication, you'd be well up on. Can't run it this month and it'll need legalling. Writer says she'll have to check with her sources but it's an interesting piece.'

I took the sheets and looked at the top page. The article was headed: EARTHQUAKE VICTIM? The writer was Helen Broadway.

3

Helen had written three pages setting out Horrie Jacobs' story pretty much as he'd told it to me without the embellishments. A few quotes were included: 'If that wasn't Oscar then it was someone who looked like him and moved like him and wore the same sort of cap. And that cap was the only one of its kind in captivity.' I'd have to ask about the cap. Some of the piece was in point form—questions, assumptions. Helen had attached a note to Harry stressing that it was a rough draft which needed a lot more work. She wondered if he was interested.

When I looked up from the pages Harry was staring at me as if I was growing wings. 'Are you?' I said.

'What?'

'Interested. Apart from the prurient curiosity, I mean.'

'Dunno,' Harry said. 'Reckon there's anything in it?'

'Could be. This guy Jacobs has hired me to look into it.'

21

On Helen's recommendation?'

I nodded. 'Don't make anything of it, Harry. She's just doing her job. Tell you one thing she hasn't mentioned though.' I was suddenly reminded of Harry's ruthless methods when he was a news hound. 'Off the record.'

'I'm hurt.'

'Horrie Jacobs won the Lotto a few years back. He's loaded.'

Harry put his Nikes up on the desk. Since he quit wearing a suit he never wears anything else on his feet but sneakers. I think he'd wear them with a suit if he ever had to go formal again. 'Now that *is* interesting,' he said. 'D'you think it's some kind of scam to get at his loot?'

'I hope you don't let your writers use language like that.'

He grinned. 'Can't help it—private eye on a big case, big money and a woman . . . '

He let the last word hang in the air. Harry had liked Helen enormously and told me I was a fool to let her go. I told him it wasn't exactly like that—more a matter of being wrenched apart, but he'd seen me stumbling around emotionally ever since and was too good a friend not to hope for something better for me. I said I'd keep him posted. Pauline yelled from across the room that she couldn't keep holding off Harry's calls any longer. Harry hit a button on his handset and picked up the phone.

I went over to the bench and began to work through the *Sydney Morning Herald*'s account of the earthquake and its various aftermaths. The Newcastle broadsheet would have been better but the *Challenger* didn't run to holdings of provincial papers. The pages seemed to grow heavy after a while: my mind wasn't completely on the job. The thought that Horrie Jacobs was the target for some kind of confidence operation had occurred to me. It happens. People who get rich quick get blackmailed, kidnapped, threatened, tricked. For years after they have their stroke of luck they are besieged by begging letters and the creators of sure-fire schemes to double the winners' money, who just need a little seed capital. It was something to consider along with the question of Horrie's eyesight and mental state, the possibility of aftershocks and delayed wall-collapses. Also whether the body over which the inquest was held really was that of Oscar Bach. And who was he, anyway? Then there was the question of the involvement of Helen Broadway and whether we might be in what the sportscasters called a team situation, here.

After an hour with the papers and photocopier I had a solid press record on the earthquake, the disputes between the rescue services, the conflicts between the conservationists and developers, the fund raising and the inquests on the dead. I put five dollars on Pauline's desk. She shook her head and tried to give it back to me.

'I'm on expenses,' I said.

Harry moved his mouth away from the phone. 'Take it,' he said.

I gave them all a general wave goodbye and left the office. The ones that noticed smiled and waved back. A happy bunch. As I got into the lift I realised that I was feeling pretty happy myself.

Back in Darlinghurst I collected the Falcon from the all-day car park that charges me more than I can afford. In the old days I parked my car on a cement slab made available to me by a tattooist in exchange for letting him share vicariously in the thrills of my profession. There never were many thrills, but now there's no slab and no tattooist. The area's changing—a one-time wine bar is now a fantasy lingerie shop, yesterday's crumbling student slum is today's smart financial consultant's office. Depressing, especially if you've got no need for either service. I drove home to Glebe thinking about the time I bought Cyn, my ex-wife, a black silk nightgown in David Jones and how she'd exchanged it for something else.

My work lately, before the present extremely dry spell, had consisted mainly of bodyguarding, interviewing witnesses to motor accidents and locating defaulters on maintenance payments. It was nice to have a case on hand with some corners and blind alleys. By the time I reached Glebe I'd succeeded in putting the past out of my mind and focussing on the future. I had a drink in the Toxteth and agreed that Balmain weren't travelling too well. My drinking companion was Carl, who used to be called the Prince of the Anarchists before his heart attack. He was fifty-five and looked seventy.

'Light beer's tasting stronger and old sheilas are looking younger,' Carl said.

Even that couldn't depress me. I shopped for the usual things and let myself into the house prepared for the brief, supercilious company of the cat. I'd feed it and myself out of tins and virtuously read over the photocopies and review the Jacobs case. The phone was ringing insistently when I entered the house. I hadn't switched on the answering machine. That piece of carelessness threatened my good temper. I dumped the plastic bags on the floor and grabbed the phone.

'Cliff Hardy.'

'Mr Hardy. My name is Ralph Jacobs. I'm Horace Jacobs' son and I'd very much like to have a talk with you.'

The voice was smooth and calm, well used to phrases such as 'very much like'. He didn't sound a bit like his old man. 'I'm not sure, Mr Jacobs,' I said. 'What would you like to talk about?'

'I think you know that.'

'I'm certainly not going to discuss a client's business over the phone.'

A note of impatience crept in. 'Fair enough. I understand you're meeting Dad in Hamilton tomorrow?'

I didn't say anything, but I liked 'Dad' better than 'my father'.

'I rang him this afternoon and he told me, you see. He's not a well man, Mr Hardy. I really think we should have a talk before you take this any further.'

If Horrie Jacobs had told his son about our meeting, that let me off the hook. Maybe Ralph could give me something useful. I told him I was driving up to Newcastle in the morning but that I could let him have half an hour beforehand.

'When?' he said.

'Nine o'clock, in Darlinghurst.' I gave him the address.

'I have to come in from French's Forest.'

'Nice early start for you, Mr Jacobs. See you at nine.'

I poured a small scotch, flooded it with soda water, told myself that it was infantile to want to put something in my mouth, set fire to it and give myself lung cancer, and sat down with the earthquake clippings. It was almost as if the papers had followed an even-handed policy—the accounts of people crushed, trapped and buried were balanced out with stories of near misses, miraculous escapes and heroism. For Australia, it was a major disaster. The Workers' Club on the corner of King and Union Streets had folded like a card house; several floors had collapsed down into the car park. Nine dead, dozens injured. Photographs showed Beaumont Street, Hamilton, looking like a war zone. Buildings had fallen as if they had been bombed; three people had died when shop awnings and rubble had fallen on them. Many more had been injured.

In the case of the Workers' Club there looked to be a fair degree of human error. The building wasn't old, not the part that had suffered most damage. There were questions raised about the suitability of some of the construction methods. There were ifs and buts about the Beaumont Street structures, too. Were the tie-rods supporting the awnings properly anchored? Had renovations and tartings-up weakened the fronts of the buildings? But in Hamilton the main problem appeared to be geological. The area was a flood plain and Beaumont Street itself was an old bed of the Hunter River. Its basic composition was sand, and when the quake struck it shook like jelly on a plate.

The shock had hit buildings sacred and profane—the Workers' Club, the Newcastle RSL Club, the Kent Hotel, several schools, community centres and churches. Oscar Bach had allegedly died when a section of the wall of the Holy Cross church had fallen on him as he was preparing to treat the church's foundations with a pest control chemical. There were other casualties away from the centre of destruction, spreading out into the nearby towns and suburbs like aftershocks. A locally renowned musician had died after the evacuation of the hospital where he had undergone an operation; a hospitalised woman whose condition may have been aggravated by the earthquake also died. There were several traffic accidents attributable to the quake. Horrie Jacobs himself could be considered a victim.

I'd experienced a few earth tremors myself—
in the Solomon Islands where I'd been investi-
gating an insurance fraud and on the south
coast where I'd been holidaying with Cyn in
one of our many failed efforts to keep the
marriage together. I remembered swaying
lights, falling books, spilled drinks and the
startled barking of dogs, but nothing like this.
For weeks people all over Sydney were
inspecting their houses for cracks. We got
a lot of heavy rain early in the year and
people complained about leaks caused by the
tremor. I didn't. I knew I had leaks before the
quake. On December 28 at 10.27 I'd been
swimming in the Leichhardt municipal pool
and hadn't felt a thing. I'd written the earthquake off as one of those disasters that
hadn't touched me. But now it had. It couldn't
have been easy for Horrie Jacobs to consult
me with his private problem that no-one
wanted to hear about. Maybe it wasn't easy
for Helen Broadway to give him my name, to
probe at that wound.

It was all very interesting, something to think
about while I put the cat out and had another
weak scotch. I took the dregs of the drink up to
bed along with Larry McMurtry's *Lonesome
Dove*, sure to take care of my reading needs for
at least a month. I finished the drink and read
about Cal and Gus and Jake and the pigs until I
was sleepy. I put the book down and turned off
the light. I knew what would happen. It was an
unfailing pattern. I'd sleep for three hours, get

up and piss and drink weak instant coffee and read and sleep some more. There's a line in a Dire Straits song that says it all—'You know it's evil when you're livin' alone.' Right on, Mark.

4

Ralph Jacobs resembled his father the way a dog resembles a duck. He was well over six feet tall and fleshy. His barbering and tailoring suggested vanity and he had the good manners of a man who has worked at having good manners. I'd beaten him to the office by about five minutes, giving me the moral edge. I had a feeling I was going to need every advantage I could find. I ushered him into the chair his father had sat in and took up my position behind the desk. My manners aren't so good—I looked at my watch.

'It's good of you to see me,' Ralph said. 'But I think you'll find it worthwhile. I won't beat about the bush, Mr Hardy, my father's mental state isn't the best.'

'Whose, Mr Jacobs?'

'I'm glad you can see the amusing side of an old man's deterioration.'

'I can see the amusing side of someone calling gaga a bloke who struck me as very sharp and well in control of himself. And as a very nice man, too, by the way.'

'He is a nice man and I'm very fond of him. That's why I don't want to see him distressed. And I have my mother to think of, as well.'

'He didn't say anything about his wife being sick.'

'She isn't.'

'Then I don't see your problem. Your father came to me with a matter that I'm equipped to handle . . . '

'For a fee.'

'Of course. What do you do for a living, Mr Jacobs?'

He looked surprised at the question. 'I run a chain of sporting goods stores. Also I manage the Chargers.'

That explained his surprise. I recognised him now. 'Wrecker' Jacobs, who'd played Rugby League for Newcastle and regularly put city players in hospital in the the city versus country games. He'd refused all offers to play in the city competition and had only come to Sydney as a businessman and team manager. I hadn't seen a photograph of the Wrecker since his playing days and he'd gained a good deal of weight and lost some hair. 'I've placed you,' I said. 'Chargers aren't doing so good, are they?'

Jacobs eyed me now with frank dislike. 'I did some checking around on you before I came here,' he said. 'I've got a few mates on the force and in your game, too.'

'You would have.'

'There's those who say you're honest and get the job done and some who reckon you're a smartarse fuck-up.'

'You can't please everybody,' I said.

'Right now, I'm leaning to the smartarse point of view. You must be pretty desperate to take this case on. Haven't you got anything better to do?'

'Such as what?'

I put a bit of an edge on the question and Jacobs had obviously done enough deals in his life to smell one when it started to cook. He unbuttoned the jacket of his double-breasted grey pinstripe and let a little flesh breathe. 'I could put some work your way . . . '

He stopped when he saw me grinning. He knew he'd been had. It made him angry. His already high colour mounted. 'You bloody low-life loser. What a dump. What sort of a business could be run from here?'

'I don't run it from here really,' I said. 'I run it out on the street and in pubs and other places where people talk to me and tell me things I need to know. Right now, I'd like to know why a prosperous business gentleman like yourself is worried about his father wanting to find out what happened to his friend.'

Ralph snorted. 'Friend!'

'That's what he called him. Do you say something different?'

'It was a matter of time. The man was a crook. He was just waiting to take Dad for everything he had.'

'I understood they were friends from before your father got rich.'

'Did Dad tell you that?'

32

'I'd have to check my notes, but that's my impression.'

'That's bullshit. Bach hardly knew Dad before he won the Lotto. Then he moved in on him—"Let's go fishing, Horrie," and "Beer is for birdbrains, Horrie." I tell you he was getting set.'

There was malice in Jacobs' voice, but also concern. He was aware that he was revealing more of his feelings than he'd intended and he reined back. 'All this stuff about him not getting killed in the earthquake is crap. Dad got concussed and he can't think straight. Drop it.'

I shook my head. 'I can't do that. I've taken his money.'

'And you plan to take a hell of a lot more of it.'

'I think you'd better go, Mr Jacobs, before this gets nast*. You don't look like much of a wrecker to me now. You should turn out with the team now and then, get a bit of the flab off.'

He half rose from his chair and his clothes suddenly weren't fitting him so well. He had the hunched shoulders and corded neck of the front-row brawler. But he was a smart man who'd learned what a bad play physical violence was. He sat back and drew in a deep breath. 'One of my police mates said you had something called ethics.'

'He must've looked it up in his pocket Macquarie.'

Jacobs cleared his throat. 'I can see that you plan to go through with this. Go up to Newcastle, see Dad, sniff around.'

33

'That's right.'

'Okay. Maybe it's for the best. Maybe when you tell him there's nothing in it he'll let it lie.'

I shrugged. 'Who knows?'

He got up and loomed over the desk, buttoning up the double-breaster. 'I'll just say this. I've got a lot of friends in Newcastle. Good blokes—cops, miners, football players.'

'I'm glad,' I said. 'Must be nice to have some mates to drink with after you've dropped in on the old dad and mum. How long's it been, Wrecker?'

That went home. He wanted to hit me. He wanted to break something, but he didn't. He showed his even, capped teeth in a smile that had all the warmth of a packet of frozen peas. 'Just watch yourself up in Newcastle, smartarse,' he said.

I'd driven through and around Newcastle often enough over the past few years in my assaults on, and retreats from, Helen Broadway, but it had been ten years or more since I'd actually set a course for the city intending to do work there. The drive up the freeway is untesting and the rivers and ranges and glimpses of Lake Macquarie are easy on the eye. As drives in Australia go, the one from Sydney to Newcastle is calculated to allow you to arrive in a reasonably good mood. North of Belmont I noted the turn-off to Redhead and Dudley. I had an overnight bag on the front seat sitting on top of a manilla folder with the Jacobs case materials as assembled so far. I also had a camera, a pocket-sized tape recorder and a Smith & Wesson .38. I didn't need Ralph Jacobs to tell me that Newcastle was a tough town where Sydneysiders can be thought of as invaders from another planet.

Signs of the earthquake began in Broadmeadow—vacant blocks, braces holding up brick walls, scaffolding and tarpaulin-shrouded buildings—and increased closer to Hamilton. Beaumont Street had been considerably cleaned up, but there were still some shells of buildings, scars where awnings had fallen and braces, scaffolds and tarps. The Kent Hotel had been a victory for the conservationists. The building, which had lost almost its entire front wall, was in the process of renovation. Several empty blocks, scoured down to the sandy earth, indicated where the developers had won.

I parked opposite a collection of bricks and metal that had once been a chemist shop, to judge from the remnants of the paintwork. It was five minutes to midday. That's Hardy, compulsively early yet again. The day was mild, with a clear sky and a light wind keeping the temperature down. It might have been my imagination, but I fancied that some of the shoppers glanced up apprehensively at the awnings over the pavement and that more than a few of them kept to the roadway as much as they could. Dust from the reconstruction work going on hung in the air. The earthquake was still very much a presence in Beaumont Street.

At noon precisely Horrie Jacobs appeared from around the corner to stand outside the Kent Hotel. I was parked about sixty metres away on the other side of the road, giving him a test. He passed it. He took off his sunglasses, shaded his eyes, looked up and down the street and spotted me. Pretty good for nearly seventy in a busy street. I got out of the car, crossed the road and we met outside a boarded-up shopfront. We shook hands. Horrie was wearing a polo shirt with an insignia on the pocket, cotton slacks and canvas shoes. He smelled slightly of aftershave and his face was scraped very close. Professional job.

'It's a mess, isn't it?'

I nodded. 'The insurance companies couldn't have been too happy.'

'They've been pretty good, most of 'em. My place down the road got a bit of a hammering and the insurance came good. I haven't heard too many complaints.'

'Could you show me where everything happened?'

We walked south along the street, away from the concentration of shops. Horrie stopped at a corner and pointed down a curving, tree-lined street. 'Gollan Street. See the little joint there, the white one?'

I looked at a narrow-fronted cottage with a minute front garden and an iron roof, the back part of which was weathered and the front, brand, spanking new. The other houses in the

36

street bore similar signs of recent work. I nodded, thinking that Horrie and his son the Wrecker had come a long way from their humble beginnings.

'My place. Can't bear to sell it, so I rent it to a bloke like I told you. Well, I'd just come away after having a cuppa and a yarn and I came up to here and went along a bit.'

We moved along the street until we were opposite an imposing brick church occupying a corner block on the other side of the road. A huge tarpaulin draped one side of it and there were piles of bricks and timber stacked on the nature strip of the side street.

Horrie pointed. 'Foundations on that side at the back fell in. Took the whole of the . . . dunno what you call it, the sticking out bit, down with 'em. They found Oscar there, about where you see that cement mixer, but in among the bricks.'

The machine was inside the low wall that ran around the church. A section of tarpaulin flapped near it. I could see a yellow hard hat sitting on top of the drum.

'But . . . ' I said.

'But I saw him out on the street looking at the damage a couple of minutes later. Bricks had fallen right out on the road, bounced around and that. But Oscar was there, in his blue overall, still carrying something in his hand.'

'What was he carrying?'

'I couldn't see. This was all over in a matter of seconds, you understand. The window of that

37

shop there,' he pointed to a large tinted window, 'had fallen right out and I could see what had happened further up the street. Sounded like a bomb had gone off. People were screaming and there was a dust cloud starting to go up above the building level.'

'No dust here?'

'Fair bit, but not enough to stop me seeing what I saw. The whole of that part of the church was down and Oscar was standing clear of it. I might've waved at him, I don't know. I know he saw me, but.'

'How did you come to be at this spot?'

'Didn't I say? I was looking out for Oscar. I wanted him to take a look at the house. Thought it might need a treatment. I knew he was doing the church that morning and thought I might be able to grab him.'

'Uh huh.' I didn't know whether that was good news or bad. A psychologist might say that the expectation had been realised in the mind rather than in reality.

'Anyway,' Horrie continued, 'I scooted along to my car. It was parked back there.'

He pointed back towards Gollan Street.

'And I took off hell for leather for home. Do you want to go and take a closer look at the church?'

'Later,' I said. 'How far did you get, Mr Jacobs?'

A bit of the bounce went out of him. 'Adamstown. I hit another car as I told you. My fault, I suppose. They took my licence away. May has to drive me around now. It's a bloody

38

nuisance. There's nothing wrong with me. I can still drive.'

There was a querulous note in his voice, the first time he had sounded anything but firm and confident. I took another look at the place, peaceful and quiet now but a scene of flying bricks and shattered glass back then. There were six houses placed so as to give a view of the side of the church. I asked Horrie Jacobs whether he had sought confirmation of his account from the residents.

He shook his head. 'Never thought of it.'

'Do you think the police would have talked to them?'

'Not them. No chance! Want to try it now?'

'That's my job. You're paying me to do it. What're your plans now?'

'Nothing much.' He looked at his watch. 'May's picking me up in twenty minutes. Do you want to come out to Dudley?'

'No. I've got a few things to do here and in Newcastle first. Would it be all right if I came out later this afternoon?'

'For sure. Not a fisherman by any chance, are you?'

I shook my head. 'I've never caught a fish in my life.'

'Pity. Well, I'll see you at home later. And thanks, Mr Hardy.'

'Cliff,' I said.

He nodded and walked off, a small figure holding himself very straight, but not quite the man I imagined him as being back on December 28.

39

I ran my fingers through my hair and did up a button of my shirt. I was wearing drill trousers and my old but smart Italian leather shoes. I didn't look like Richard Gere, but I wasn't Charlie Chaplin either. I got out a notebook and pen and my Private Enquiry Agent's licence and approached the first of the six houses, a wide fronted Federation job with windows that looked directly onto the collapsed side of Holy Cross church. I opened the gate, and walked up the path, keeping an eye and ear out for a dog. No dog. No-one home either.

At the next two houses I drew blanks. The women who spoke to me at the door seemed relieved that I hadn't come to take money from them but couldn't offer any help—not at home, or not looking in the direction of the church at the time. The fourth house had the best view of the destruction; light glinted on french windows looking out across a patio and a low fence towards the church.

I went up the steps to the front of the house but I didn't have to knock. The door was opened and a woman stood framed against the light. She had a cigarette in the hand she used to open the screen door and a drink in the other hand. Welcoming.

'Saw you going into those other houses,' she said. 'Knew you'd be coming here.'

I showed her the licence. She drew on the cigarette and puffed smoke over my shoulder. She was tall and lean, wearing a singlet top and shorts. Bare feet.

'I'd like to ask you a few questions about

40

what happened when the church was damaged,' I said. 'That is, if you were here.'

She moved her thin body aside to let me pass by her into the house, although I could have made it easily. She stayed propped up against the door and I had the feeling that she'd touch the wall all the way down the passage. Either that or grab me for support. She was a good-looking, thirty-five-ish woman with short dark hair and glazed blue eyes. She was very drunk. 'Insurance,' she said.

'No. I'm a private detective. I'm making enquiries about the death . . .

She took a risk, moved away from the door-jamb and grabbed my arm. The cigarette threatened to burn a hole in my shirt sleeve. 'Come in,' she slurred, 'it's about time someone looked into this.'

5

She walked with unnatural steadiness down the dark passageway towards the light. She grabbed at the door that led through to the kitchen and I'd have bet there was a mark on the wood at just that spot from all the other times before. The kitchen was modern and dirty. The polished floorboards were sticky and there were glasses and mugs all over the sink and a few more of each on the table. There was no sign of solid food ever being consumed. She made straight for the bench where a four-litre cask of white wine was sitting precariously near the edge. On the floor beneath it was a thick puddle that had attracted flies and dust.

She dropped her still-burning cigarette into the sink and, without consulting me, took a glass from beside the sink. She ran water into it, swilled it out, and filled it to the brim from the cask. Then she filled her own. 'Have a drink.'

I took the glass, feeling the slippery, greasy surface and wondering how long since it had seen hot water.

'Let's go outside.'

The french windows were open. She made it through them with inches to spare on one side and flopped down on a banana lounge, the metal legs of which moved and scratched the patio's tiles, not for the first time. I sat opposite her in a canvas deckchair. She lifted her glass carefully to her mouth; her breasts rose under her singlet and the thin roll of fat around her waist tensed. She drank and the flesh subsided. 'I didn't get your name?'

'Cliff Hardy. From Sydney.' I don't know why I said that, possibly because I thought she might talk more freely to someone who wasn't going to be around to talk about her.

She grinned sloppily and sang, in a passable imitation of the voice that used to close down one of the Sydney TV stations each night, back when the stations closed: '*My city of Syd-ney, I've never been a-way*. Great town, better than this hole.'

I got out my notebook, allowing me to put the dirty glass of warm wine down on the tiles. 'Mrs . . . ?'

'Atkinson, Rhonda Atkinson, formerly of Sydney, now of Shitville.'

'You said there was reason to enquire about the damage to the church.'

'That's right. Finally getting the message, are they?' She drank half of her glass in two gulps and waved her hand at the kitchen. 'Would you get my smokes? They're in there somewhere.'

I went into the kitchen and looked around

43

among the debris. A packet of Sterling ultra-milds and a disposable lighter lay on a shelf above the sink along with an array of about twenty bottles with labels detailing the prescribed doses. 'The capsules, for depression'; 'the tablets, for sleeplessnness', 'the tonic ...' They were all prescribed for Mrs R. Atkinson and they did not make me feel hopeful. None of the labels recommended that they be taken with liberal quantities of cheap wine.

I took the cigarettes out to Mrs Atkinson. She flipped the box open and pulled one free with a practised pout of her full lips. I lit it for her.

'Want one?'

I shook my head and went back to the chair.

'Wowser, are you? Don't drink neither?'

I couldn't have that. I grabbed the glass and took a decent swig. I'd drunk it warmer and worse in my time, much worse. 'Tell me about the church, Mrs Atkinson.'

She finished off her drink and rested the empty glass on her slight stomach roll. She blew smoke in the direction of Holy Cross. 'My husband's under there,' she said, 'only they won't bloody-well admit it.'

Rhonda Atkinson was convinced, or pretended to be convinced, that her husband was beneath the collapsed foundations of the church across the road. To the suggestion that the wreckage had been cleared and only one body discovered she said, 'Huh, with bloody great scoops and shovels as big as a room. They must've missed

44

him. Dumped him in a truck like garbage.' She knew nothing about Oscar Bach and cared less. She had not been at home when the earthquake struck. It took half an hour and lot of phony note scribbling and head nodding and the finishing off of the glass of warm white to get away from her.

I drove slowly around Hamilton thinking that the earthquake had claimed more victims than people realised. Mrs Atkinson was another one. Her kind is always produced by natural or man-made disasters. Ask around after any revolution and you'll find wives whose husbands have seized the chance to slip away. The town was battered all right, almost every big building showed signs of damage. There must have been a lot of closing down sales and dust-damaged goods going cheap. Big, solid trees grew along the roads and in the parks; I thought of their roots going down and wrapping around house-sized boulders under the ground, gripping the bedrock. It made the 180-year-old city seem very impermanent.

Long and painful experience has taught me that the first thing to do when arriving in a town and preparing to annoy the citizens is to check in first with the cops. Newcastle is a nicely laid out place, a sort of ribbon running along a narrow spit of land with water—the Pacific Ocean and the Hunter River—on both sides. The Police Headquarters was on the corner of Church and Watt Streets, and my Gregory's showed me how handy everything was for the authorities—the court house, a hospital and the

morgue were all nearby. I parked legally, beginning as I meant to go on, and walked a couple
of blocks to the police station. Nice wide
streets, solid buildings; it must have filled the
convicts with pride to have hacked all this out
of the swamp and scrub.

No-one at Police HQ was overly impressed
by my credentials, but they didn't kick me
down the steps. After some sitting, thumb twid-
dling and yawning in a waiting room that was
about one step above a lockup for comfort, I
was shown into the presence of Detective
Inspector Edward Withers. That's what it said
on the nameplate on his desk. He didn't look
up from his paperwork, just pointed to a chair
and said, 'Ticket'.

I put the licence on the desk just out of his
reach and sat down. He continued to flick
through papers and make notes. I sat. To look at
the licence he'd have to stop paper shuffling.
Balding head hunched over, wide shoulders,
shirt sleeves, loosened tie, wedding ring glint-
ing as he methodically shifted a stack of papers
and files from his left to his right. To talk to him
would be like talking to a hay bailer. War of
nerves.

Eventually he had transferred every sheet and
folder from one side to the other. Had to do
something with those big, meaty hands. He
reached for the licence, glanced at it and dropped it as if it was something that needed wiping.

'What're you doing here, Hardy?'

The voice, coming out of a face that looked
as if it had been kicked more often than kissed,

was what you'd expect, a deep, don't-bullshit-me rumble. I considered lying, running some line about insurance or worker's compensation, but something about his manner deterred me. He was a cop of the old school—thirty years on the force, no more corrupt than anyone else and less than some, good at scaring the shit out of ninety per cent of the crims he dealt with and probably a good family man. Tell the truth and he might co-operate, lie and be caught out and you'd lose some teeth. 'I'm working for Horrie Jacobs, Inspector,' I said. 'Know him?'

He nodded.

'He thinks a mate of his wasn't killed in the earthquake the way everyone else thinks.'

He picked up a pen and pulled a notepad closer. 'Who would that be?'

'A man named Oscar Bach.'

He dropped the pen, but I couldn't tell whether he was surprised or just uninterested. 'Inquest. Bit of a bloody church came down on him.'

'That's not what Mr Jacobs thinks.'

Withers sighed. He was bored already and I could imagine him lifting the phone and calling for another batch of papers. 'D'you know how many problems we've had to deal with this year? Dodgy insurance claims, damaged vehicles, looters, squatters . . . '

'Missing husbands,' I said.

He raised his thin, fair eyebrows. His beaten-up, ugly face didn't get any prettier but a bit more intelligence showed.

47

'I met a woman in Hamilton who's got a bee in her bonnet.'

'Rhonda Atkinson,' he said. 'Have you been bothering people already? Before checking in with us?'

First slip, Cliff, I thought. *Watch it.* 'No. We just had a chat. She did most of the talking.'

'That'd be right. Well, what does Mr Jacobs want you to do for him?'

I gave him the gist of Horrie's case, keeping it spare. I also said I'd talked to Ralph Jacobs. The name registered with him. I played it as crooked as I thought I could get away with, suggesting that I was sceptical about Horrie's story and doing the family a favour if I found nothing to support it. He listened and even made a few notes. When I'd finished, he said, 'Who can I ring in Sydney to get a reference on you? I'd prefer someone who's not in the Bay.'

Cop humour, better than no humour at all. I smiled politely. I gave him Frank Parker's name and number and stared out the window while he made the call. We were on the north side of the building and I could see out across commercial rooftops to the railway station and the harbour. It looked as if a lot of work had been done on the waterfront—I could see fresh paint and gleaming metal. The water was a deep blue and, in contrast to similar views in Sydney, the ships were cargo vessels, not a yacht in sight.

Withers put the phone down and looked at me as if I might just possibly be house-trained. 'Parker gives you a good name. He tells me you sometimes need a word, to stop you from getting yourself into trouble.'

'That's fair enough,' I said.

'We don't like extra trouble around here. We've got all we need.'

I was still gazing at the fine view. 'Looks pretty quiet to me, but you never know what you're going to find when you turn over a rock, or a brick.'

'Parker also said you liked to come the needle. I don't care for that too much.'

I looked away from the window towards the man at the desk. It was like turning off Jana Wendt and looking at the wall. 'Look, Inspector, I don't want trouble. If you can help me to get a look at the autopsy report on Bach, talk to the paramedics, tell me what the word on him was, fine. If not, I'll just quietly go through channels and knock on doors.'

He looked at my licence again, jotted a few things on his notepad and pushed the vinyl folder across the desk towards me. 'Far as I know, there was nothing about Bach to interest us. I'd be surprised if there was any sort of file on him. Migrant, I seem to remember. Ran a little business. Cleanskin. Autopsy? I dunno Did he have any family?'

'Not that I've heard of.'

'Sad, that. Family life's the only thing worth having. You got a family, Hardy?'

'No. Frank Parker's boy, Peter, is my godson. That's as close as I get.'

He frowned. 'I see. Well, the autopsy must've been done somewhere. It was all pretty chaotic

49

there at the time. I'm sure you can track it down. I can help with one thing though. I can put you in touch with the police officer who found Bach. How'd that be?'

'That'd be a big help. Who's that?'

Withers smiled, showing big, uneven, yellow teeth. 'Senior Sergeant Glenys Withers. My daughter.'

6

I suppose I'd been expecting a broad-beamed stalwart, all epaulettes and nightstick with a high-riding hip pistol. Glenys Withers was a slender woman with short brown hair and a lean, sensitive face. She was sitting behind a desk where her father said she'd be—in the personnel section, but she wasn't nearly as interested in paper shuffling as he was. She looked up as soon as I was within speaking distance. A sure sign that the person behind the desk welcomes distraction.

'Yes?' Nice voice, quiet, good-humoured, not much good for crowd-control, but it's amazing what a bullhorn can do. I was too old a hand to judge a cop by its cover.

I put my licence folder down in front of her. 'I've just been talking to Inspector Withers, upstairs, Senior,' I said. 'He recommended that I see you next.'

She examined the photo and the printed details as if she'd never seen a PEA licence before. Maybe she hadn't. Maybe she interviewed people for jobs like hers. If so, what had she been doing in Hamilton on the 28th? She closed the folder and handed it back. 'Sit down, Mr Hardy.'

She studied me with a pair of very blue eyes with a few fine lines around them that said she was thirty, not twenty. The rest of her, the hair, the nicely shaped shoulders and chest inside the crisp white shirt and the wide mouth, didn't look any particular age. Just good. I gave her a short version of the story, taking care not to sound as if the police force or anyone else had been remiss. No Royal Commission required. I tried to communicate my own interest in some of the questions that Horrie Jacobs' allegation threw up. Particularly ones he wasn't aware of, such as the notion that a rich old man was a target of some kind.

'I remember when he won all that money. Generally speaking, people said it couldn't have happened to a nicer bloke. Unusual reaction. Usually, there's jealousy.'

'He's that sort of a man,' I said.

'I don't see how I can help you, though,' she said. 'You had to be here to appreciate what things were like that day.'

'Tell me.'

'It was dreadful. We were all called out to do one thing or another. I've been on the force for ten years and I've seen a few things. But nothing like that. The distress and fear in the streets. I hope I never see it again.'

'You saw Oscar Bach's body?'

She nodded. The clean, shiny brown hair bounced. She wore two small earrings in the

lobe of one ear—a silver and a gold, inter-
locked. Somehow it made her seem less like a
police person. 'I worked in Beaumont Street,
up where the awnings had come down, for a
few hours. Then a woman said there was a body
under the church. She was hysterical. A lot of
people were. I wanted to go on helping where
I was but the Sergeant told me to go and take a
look.'

'Do you know who the woman was?'

'Yes. A Mrs Atkinson. She's got a drinking
problem. Her husband was always leaving her
and always coming back when she threatened
to kill herself, you know?'

I nodded. I knew. Who doesn't?

'She came along with me, down the street.
Weeping and carrying on. The church was a
mess. The whole of the side section had collapsed. Mr Bach was half-covered by bricks.'

'Which half?'

She looked at me with dislike and snapped,
'The top. His feet, too. Are you enjoying this? I
had a hysterical woman tearing my arm out of
the socket, blood and dust and crap all over me
and a man lying there with his head turned to
pulp. I didn't enjoy it, I can tell you.'

'I'm sorry,' I said. 'I was in a war once. I
know what you're talking about.'

'Vietnam?'

'Similar. Bit before. Malaya. It's just that I
have to be sure Oscar Bach was killed by falling
bricks, not by anything else.'

'Like what?'

I mimed the action of clutching a brick and

using it as a bludgeon. She looked at me as if she couldn't make up her mind whether I was an animal or an insect. Then she frowned. Two grooves appeared between her dark eyebrows and I had an impulse to reach across the desk and put my thumb on them, to smooth them away. 'It's possible,' she said. 'How could you tell?'

'Were there any photographs taken?'

'I don't think so. As I said, everything was chaotic. Just up the street . . . '

'Some people were killed by things falling on them. So it was assumed the same thing had happened at the church. What did Mrs Atkinson do?'

'I'm getting a bit tired of this. You're questioning my competence.'

'I have to,' I said. 'People pay me to do that. It doesn't make me popular and often I'm wrong anyway. Try to see it from my point of view.'

I liked her face, her voice and the calm steadiness of her. She was angry but not letting it block out everything else. I wondered why she was letting me take up so much of her time. I didn't kid myself it was my rugged good looks. *Dad, most likely.* She took a packet of cigarettes from her skirt pocket and offered them to me. I shook my head and she lit up. She drew on the cigarette and let the smoke out slowly. 'Mrs Atkinson waited until the paramedics came and they uncovered the body. When she saw the boots and the overall she knew it wasn't her husband and she went right off the edge. I had to take her home. They removed the body. I put in a report. That's all, Mr ... ' she butted out the cigarette.

'Hardy,' I said. 'Thank you. Do you know where the post-mortem was conducted?'

She reached for the phone on her desk. 'No, but I could find out.' She lifted the phone and dropped it. 'What the hell am I doing?'

I grinned. 'Assisting me in my enquiries. Inspector Withers cleared me with Sydney.'

'That goes without saying. He wouldn't talk to a private detective otherwise. Look, I've got work to do here and ... '

I wiped the grin and tried to look professional. 'I get the impression that you don't like people barging into town and bothering the citizens with a lot of questions. Fair enough. I wouldn't like it either if I was in your shoes. How about this? You find a few minutes in your busy day to help me—get the autopsy report, anything your people might have had on Mr Bach, a few odds and ends. You let me see them and I get out of your hair so much the quicker.'

'I don't know,' she said.

'Would you have to check with your superiors to do that?'

'No, not exactly. I was the liaison officer for the emergency unit that was set up. The one the Admiral headed up.'

'I'm told he did a great job.'

'Not bad. I think the sorts of things you want would be on file in that unit, at least temporarily. I could get them.'

55

'I'd appreciate it. Where and when could we meet?'

She consulted some scribble on a scratch pad. 'I still don't know why I'm doing this. I could find some time later this afternoon . . . I have to be in court tomorrow morning . . .'

It wasn't the best arrangement because it gave her a chance to consult with her Dad, but it was the best I was going to get. 'Outside the court house? Tomorrow at 12.30?'

'All right.'

I thanked her and left the office, feeling her eyes on my back every step of the way.

For the next hour or so I confirmed my impression that good things had been done on the Newcastle waterfront and at the train terminal. A pedestrian mall had been constructed with walkways leading up over the tracks to restaurants, shops and pleasant spots for just sitting and looking beside the water. I had a light beer and a sandwich in a cafe that afforded me a view across the Hunter River to Stockton. The price would have made old Newcastle identities like Hughie Dwyer blanch, but no-one now could eat the sort of sandwiches Hughie would have been accustomed to, so it all rinses out in the wash.

I unparked my car and drove through the streets to the site of the major earthquake disaster—the Workers' Club on the corner of King and Union Streets. The area itself surprised me; I got lost and approached along Union from the Hamilton end. I had expected a mixture of the modern plastic and the old basic, but the wide road had palm trees growing along the side and ran past a big park that looked relaxed and gracious.

I'd seen press photographs of the damage to the club but they hadn't quite prepared me for the reality. The building looked to have been a huge barn of a place, constructed in sections over time, plain to the point of ugliness. Now, it looked as if a giant fist had smashed through the roof, driving upper floors down through those below and dropping the whole lot into the underground car park. There was failed metal everywhere—steel girders twisted like spaghetti and reinforcing rods sticking out of concrete like bones poking through the skin. The whole area was surrounded by a cyclone fence and scaffolding and the demolisher's sign looked like a puny piece of boasting. In fact, demolition and reconstruction were well underway, but the site still looked as if nature rather than man was calling the shots.

I drove past the club and the fire station next door and turned into King Street. A motel sign by the side of the road reminded me of that practical necessity. I turned off into a street that climbed a hill and located the motel near the crest. The Hillside, what else? It commanded a view of the city and the water and it had a pool. Lotto winners have to spend their money somehow. I booked in and swam several laps of the somewhat murky pool, which isn't as impressive as it sounds—it was about ten metres long.

After a shower and a can of beer from the minibar, I fell asleep on the bed. My last thought was of the chevrons on Glenys Withers' crisp, white shirtsleeve. Kiss me goodnight, Senior Sergeant.

I woke up about five o'clock with the late afternoon sun streaming into the small, warm room. As often happens, I woke with questions in my head. This time they were what happened to Oscar Bach's business and who wound up his affairs? Probably some solicitor in Newcastle. I reproached myself—I could have been doing something useful instead of sleeping. I took my notebook and the Gregory's for Newcastle and environs and set out for Dudley.

I became aware of the car following me soon after making the turn off from the highway to Kahiba. Bad move, to leave the main road when you're the subject of possible hostile attention, but there it was. The tail was a dark, anonymous-looking sedan—a bad sign. Amateurs follow people and commit crimes in red Alfas, people who know what they're about, don't. I drove along the narrow road with the forest on either side, speeding up just a bit to make sure I was the subject. I was. The dark car stayed with me. I slowed down and two other cars pulled out and passed me and the tail. Now it was just us and I wasn't in the mood. I gunned the motor and decided to make a race of it through this section to Whitebridge where

58

it looked as if there might be more people around.

The Falcon was in good order and speedy. I was pulling away from what I decided was a Toyota when I saw the level crossing ahead. My reaction was purely instinctive. I hit the brakes and went into the sort of skidding slide that slows down time. When I was young there were a lot of these crossings around Sydney and people got killed at them regularly. I could remember front-page newspaper pictures of the tangled wrecks and blood-daubed victims. These pictures were going through my head as I fought the skid, strained my ears for the sound of a train and kept my eyes on the rear vision mirror.

I stopped the skid and the car just before the crossing and needed a fraction of a second to be sure that the line was clear. I didn't get it. The Toyota slewed past me in a controlled glide and stopped with its front bumper inches away from mine. Another movement from either vehicle and the road would be littered with broken glass and plastic. For no good reason, something Helen Broadway had once said came into my head, 'Bourgeois love of property affects all classes.' I swore and rammed the gear shift into first, ready to plough forward, when I felt and heard the window by my right ear shatter. Glass showered in on me as I threw myself across to the other side of the bench seat. The Falcon stalled and so did I.

I could feel the blood on my face, just like those victims of thirty years before. I scrabbled

59

for the Colt I kept in a clip under the dashboard before I remembered that I didn't have it there anymore. It was in the cupboard under the stairs in Glebe. New car, the quiet life. My Smith & Wesson was in the glove box. I heaved myself back at the driver's side door, determined to do something.

'Fuck you,' a voice said. 'I've got your fuckin' blood all over me.'

He was big, carrying what looked like a short crowbar and leaning against the door. I glared at him—big, broad face, drooping moustache, weight-lifter's neck, white T shirt—all flecked with blood.

'Fuck you, too,' I said. 'Open the door and I'll bend that crowbar across your head.'

He was calm. He was good. He was very good. He said, 'The message is, watch yourself, smartarse.' He reached through the broken window and tapped me delicately on the right temple with the crowbar. The warm, bright afternoon turned to midnight.

7

I must have been out for a minute only or even less. I was aware of a face at the broken window and a voice not directed at me.

'He's alive.'

'I'm all right,' I said.

'He says he's all right.'

Another voice said, 'Let's get the fuck out of here, then.'

Young voices. Young men. Long hair, jeans and sneakers. I turned my head and saw them jump back into a Holden Commodore with several hundredweight of chrome trim. The engine roared and the Commodore took off in the direction of Whitebridge. Its rear end bucked as it jolted across the tracks. Not hard to work out—stolen car; kids with just enough conscience to take a look. I still had the tracks to cross and I wondered if I could do it.

The Falcon had stalled, so the first move wasn't too hard. Turn the key off and on again. I did that and the motor caught first time. Regular servicing, nothing like it. Then I tried getting into first gear. That worked all right so I

61

was encouraged to attempt to straighten the wheels and drive across the railway line. No problems, although the jolting was something I could have done without. I was beginning to admire the guy with the crowbar. An artist. I was coming out of the fog.fast with just a headache and a ringing in my ears to remember him by.

I drove super-cautiously to Whitebridge, always ready for the road to suddenly turn into a big dipper or end in the middle of a football ground. I'd been concussed enough times to know the tricks the brain can play. But nothing like that happened. The traffic both ways was light, the way it gets in the country when you leave the main road, and I blessed the fact. One oncoming headlight, unnecessary anyway in the evening glow and on high beam, hit me between the eyes like a stun-gun.

I made it to Whitebridge and turned onto Dudley Road running along the crest of the headland. There was sparkling, dark blue water in the distance on both sides and I felt as if I was driving along a highway that would take me all the way out to sea, maybe to Lord Howe Island. I stopped under a light, realising that the tap on the temple had affected me more than I'd thought. I consulted the Gregory's and reckoned I could set a course for Bombala Road. Why not? It wasn't nearly as far as Lord Howe Island.

I drove past the turn-off to Redhead, promising myself a look at the beach where thirty years before I'd ridden a surfboard and tried to

62

convince a local girl to come and have a holiday in Sydney with me. Dudley has two pubs which seems at least one too many for such a small place. Both pubs had cars pulled up outside them and small groups of drinkers sucking it down quietly along with the fresh sea air. Ocean Street cut the headland in two. I tried to remember the number of Oscar Bach's cottage and couldn't. Well, that's what note-taking is for. Dudley, this part of it at least, had closed down for the night. Men in singlets were watering lawns and the few elderly people sitting out on their front porches looked about ready to go in and switch on the TV. Almost every house sprouted a high mast and a set of complex antennae.

I turned into Bombala Street and saw the land fall away and the ocean spread itself out in front of me. Lights blinked on land in the far distance but I was too disoriented to know where those lights were shinin'. I was beginning to hear music in my head and I felt surprise when the car began to go faster of its own accord. I felt like saying 'Stop' but I had enough sense left to touch the brake. I stop-started down the steep street towards thick bush with the water beyond. A casual observer might have wanted to see my learner's permit; a cop would have wanted me to blow in a bag.

I stopped outside the last house in the street on the left side by jamming the car's wheels into the kerb. I got out and heard the surf crashing not too far away. The air smelled of eucalyptus and salt and cicadas started singing as soon as I slammed the car door. I walked across a wide nature strip towards a letter box that had the number 7 written on it in luminous paint. My kind of house number. I must have made it down the steps to the wide deck and all the way to the front door, but it wasn't something I was aware of at the time.

I recognised Horrie Jacobs' voice, although it was coming from far away. Then his diminuitive shape was close by and I heard a female make a noise between a gasp and a groan. Then I was sitting down somewhere quiet and warm and my head was being sponged. The female was doing the work and her hands were incredibly gentle. For some reason I preferred to keep my eyes closed.

'Mrs Jacobs?' I said.

'May. Hold steady. There's a bit of glass here wants getting out.'

I didn't feel a thing. 'You're good at this.'

'Horrie was a miner. Do you think he didn't come home with cuts and bruises under all that coal dust? You bet he did. And who fixed him up? Me, that's who.'

Horrie's voice was coming from the same hemisphere as everyone else now. 'You're right, Cliff. She is good at it.'

'You've got to be. How many times did Ralph come in after games with bits of skin hanging off him? And was Suzie all that much better?'

'Our son and second daughter,' Horrie said. 'A tomboy that Suzie.'

I nodded and regretted it. 'Did I bleed on

anything?'

'Just your shirt,' May Jacobs said. 'And I can put that in the wash.'

'What happened?' Horrie said. 'Did you run into someone?'

'Someone ran into me,' I said. 'He made his point with a crowbar, the point being not to push too hard on this enquiry of yours.'

'Told you,' May Jacobs said.

She was six or seven inches taller than him, making her a tall woman for her generation. She looked as if she'd been broadly built when younger and more active. Now she'd fined down somewhat, but she would still have out-weighed Horrie by twenty pounds. Horrie Jacobs looked at his wife. 'You didn't say anything about this sort of trouble. This backs up what *I* think. Doesn't it, Cliff?'

I was lying on a padded cane lounge in a large sitting room that seemed to have three glass walls. There was a towel under my head and the ache was easing. I sat up slowly and carefully. They'd taken off my shoes and the thick carpet under my feet felt good. Pleasant sensations were returning, always a good sign. I could think of another sensation that'd be welcome.

'Leave him alone, Horrie, I'm telling you,' May Jacobs said. I could detect the slight foreign sound in her voice for the first time. 'Poor man's had a terrible knock. Would you like a cup of tea, Mr Hardy?'

It was about the last thing I wanted and it must have shown in my face. Horrie chuckled.

65

'He needs something stronger than that, love. Hang on.'

He went quickly out of the room and I felt I had to apologise. I'd seen ex-boozers seize a chance to start again before, any chance. 'Tea'd be fine, Mrs Jacobs,' I said. 'I don't want . . . '

'Hush. He knows what he's doing. Are you well enough to talk? We're going to have to thrash this out.'

Horrie came back before I could answer. He had a big brandy in a wine glass and he gave it to me. 'That'll see you right. Good stuff that, they tell me. Ralph brought it back from some trip or other.'

I touched my face and could feel where blood had crusted on some cuts. I sipped the brandy and then had a solid slug. Good stuff? It was Grade A Cognac and it seemed to run through every blood vessel to soothe all the parts that hurt. May went off to make tea for Horrie and herself and I looked around the room while I worked on the brandy. Big, cane furniture, carpet, huge windows. There was a large bookcase filled with a variety of books stacked in as if they were there to be read and looked at instead of displayed. There were cushions and magazines lying around. A couple of broad-leafed plants sprouted from earthernware pots. The fireplace was big and, to judge from the slight smoke stains on the wall and roof above it, got plenty of use in the winter. It was a nice, plain room. Horrie Jacobs watched me survey his domain.

'Doesn't look like a millionaire's place, does

it? Ralph's always at me to do it up but I dunno, it suits May and me.'

'I think it's fine. Which way's the water?'

He pointed to a window that was filled with points of light I took to be stars. 'Thataway. View'll knock your eyes out in the morning. Oh, sorry, that's not the best thing to say.' He leaned forward and examined my battered head. 'Didn't miss your eye by that much. I'd better ring the police.'

'No, I've already seen the police and got some co-operation. I don't want to muddy the waters with them.' I waved the glass at him thinking that he might take the hint and give me a refill but he didn't move. 'I'm OK. I was careless. I think you're right—there is something behind Oscar Bach's death, but . . . '

May came back into the room carrying a tray with two mugs of tea, a plate of biscuits and a bottle of Panadol tablets on it. She put the tray on the floor and pulled up one of the heavy cane chairs with a quick, strong heave. Her broad face was framed by a floating wreath of white hair. Her dark eyes, slightly slanted and deep, fixed me. 'Look up,' she said, 'look down, left, right. How old are you? Where are you right now?'

I did all these things, told her how old I was and finished with, 'At 7 Bombala Road, Dudley.'

'Street,' Horrie said.

I was still extending the glass in his direction. 'Near enough. D'you think I could have a little more brandy?'

'That'd be all right,' May said. Horrie left the

room and she spoke urgently. 'I didn't like that Oscar. There was something ... wrong about him. Horrie couldn't see it. I'm Polish. I've seen a lot of things you wouldn't believe and heard about a lot more. If he got killed by someone I wouldn't be surprised, but I can't see what it's got to do with my Horrie. He's not young and not as strong as he looks. I don't want him to be upset, you understand me?'

I was getting confused: Horrie was coming at me from one direction; May from another and Ralph, maybe Ralph, from yet another. A family affair. The worst kind. Perhaps Suzie and her sisters'd want to put their oars in, too. Horrie gave me another, smaller, brandy and I sipped it while they drank their tea and the stars twinkled outside the window.

I heard Horrie say, 'He was a good mate, love. He didn't mind that I wouldn't go to the pub. He never asked for a penny off me.'

May said, 'I know, but Polish women have feelings about these things ... '

'Think of the fish we caught. How he cleaned them for you.'

'Fish are free from the ocean.'

'It takes skill to catch them. A good fisherman's a good bloke, I always say.'

May gave me a despairing look. They'd had this talk a hundred times before. I was intensely interested in her instinct and feelings. I had another woman working for me, I seemed to remember. What was her name? Helen? No, Glenys ... I drank the brandy which suddenly smelled and tasted of sex, of sweat, massage oil and the other good things.

'Get the glass and move the cushions, Horrie,' May said. 'He's dropping off. I'll get a blanket.'

I said, 'I'm at a motel . . .

I felt something soft cover me and I heard May's voice. 'Not tonight you're not, Mr Tough Guy.'

8

Sometime during the night one of the Jacobses must have looked in on me. There was a glass of water on a low table near the couch. I swilled it down my parched throat and lay back wondering how I'd ever got up at dawn to surf, or to go on jungle patrols or drive from Sydney to Kempsey ... Well, that hadn't been so long ago. The room was dim but I could tell there was a very bright day out behind the heavy drapes. I'd lost one sock during the night and one of my feet was cold. I swung my feet clear of the blanket and tested the strength in my legs by just putting them on the carpet and pressing down a little. Not bad. Might even be able to stand up if I had another glass of water.

It was 6.30 and the house was quiet. It isn't too polite to go prowling through people's homes that early, but what does the bladder know about manners? I went as quietly and directly as I could to the toilet—that is, I made a couple of wrong turnings and and found an en suite bathroom off one of the bedrooms. It was a big house, fairly new and furnished in a plain style that harked back to an earlier period. I examined myself in the mirror and didn't much like what I saw—stubble, scabs forming on half a dozen facial cuts. The iridologist who used to work in my building once looked at me professionally, clucked her tongue and shook her head. I don't think she would've liked the look of my eyes this morning. When I came out of the toilet I could hear noises that suggested coffee and fruit juice, maybe even aspirin.

Horrie Jacobs, wearing navy blue pyjamas and a white silk dressing gown, was making tea in the kitchen. In my crumpled pants and one sock he made me feel like a tramp.

Nothing wrong with his hearing. He swung around before my bare foot squeaked on the lino tiles. 'Cliff, I was going to see if you wanted anything. How're you feeling?'

It wasn't a comfortable situation. I was supposed to be the tough, capable professional and here was this old guy, and a client at that, nursemaiding me. It made me surly. I sat down at the kitchen table. 'I'm OK, Horrie. Any chance of some coffee?'

He nodded and included a cup of instant in his preparations. He didn't speak. He put the coffee and a carton of milk in front of me and went off with the tea tray. When he came back he put my shirt, which had been washed, over a chair. 'Guest bathroom's at the back. Towels and a razor should be there. See you in half an hour.'

He did when I was showered, shaved and dressed and in a better mood. I had another cup of coffee and felt human again. Horrie was dressed in shorts, T shirt and sneakers. He looked a little like Harry Hopman. May didn't emerge and Horrie said she liked to sleep in. 'Got bugger all chance to when the kids were around and I was working.'

I nodded. 'Are you planning on going fishing or what?'

He grinned. 'Don't know much about fishing do you?'

'No.'

'Too bright now. Have to get down early. Fish don't like the sunlight. Anyway, I haven't done much since Oscar died.'

There was a sad eagerness in him and I realised he expected to tag along with me at whatever I was going to do. That'd be all right for now, but not for long. I asked him about Oscar Bach's estate and business.

'Funny that,' he said. 'I didn't find a will.'

'*You* didn't. Wasn't there anyone handling his affairs? A solicitor or . . . '

'Nope. It was bloody strange. You couldn't really say he had any affairs. He just rented the house and ran his little business. There wasn't anyone else to do it. I went through the house and collected up his stuff. Didn't amount to much. Young bloke who worked for him part-time is sort of running the business while every-thing gets sorted out. There's some office or other handling it. I forget what it is.'

'The Public Trustee?'

'Yeah. I got a letter. I wrote back and said I didn't know anything about a solicitor or bank

72

accounts or next of kin. They said they'd let me know what happened next. But I haven't heard anything. Do you want to see the stuff?'

'Yes. Did you really search the house thoroughly?'

'Pretty well. 'Course, I'm not an expert. You can do it yourself. Place's still empty. The roof leaks and the bloody landlord hasn't got around to fixing it.' He gave a short laugh.

'What?' I said.

'Old Molly who lives next door tells everyone who comes to look at the house about the leak. She was born in the place and can't bear seeing it go to rack and ruin. She reckons if she keeps people away the landlord'll have to fix it. Worked so far and there's a fair amount of pressure on rented houses around here.'

'How's that?'

'Students from Newcastle, teachers, people wanting weekenders.' He laughed again. 'Dudley's a go ahead place. You fit for a walk?'

Outside I saw what Horrie had got for some of his winnings. His house was at the end of the street with a forest in front of it and the ocean in front of that. There was a deck around three sides and the view would be slightly different from each side—here more bushy, there more water. The garden was mostly native trees and shrubs with some landscaping—all in keeping with the plain, good taste of the whole place.

Horrie seemed to gain an inch or two when he saw me admiring the set-up. 'Not bad, eh?'

'Bloody nice. You picked a great spot.'

'Had my eye on it for years, just never had the

money. Then I did. Come on, Oscar's place's just down Ocean Street.'

We walked past a selection of houses that varied from the bookmaker-special type to the plain fibro. Many of the bigger ones had had extra storeys built to take advantage of the view. There was water on both sides—enough for everyone, but as we got closer to the top of the street the land dipped and only the houses up on pillars would have the view. Horrie set a good pace and I found my head clearing and that I was feeling better with every step. The air was cool and clean, and breathing it in deeply seemed like a good thing to do. Three doors short of the pub on the right-hand side of the street, Horrie stopped outside a small, one-pitch cottage.

'Miner's cottage,' he said. ' 'Bout eighty years old. Jesus, what's going on?'

A man, wearing overalls and swinging a hammer, came from the back of the house and walked down the narrow path towards us. The little cottage was tucked into its block with very little room to spare on either side. Looking past the man with the hammer, I could see that the land ran back a good way and rose. I wondered if there was a water view. Maybe from a few branches up in one of the big gums that grew in the yard. The man with the hammer was paying more attention to the condition of the weatherboards than to Horrie and me. After the experience of last night, that was a relief.

'Mornin', Horrie. Nice day.'

An old woman had come out of the house

next door. She was carrying the morning paper and obviously intended to sit down on her front porch. Her voice was strong and easily carried to the gate.

'Morning, Molly,' Horrie said. 'What's going on here?'

'Fixin' the house. What d'you reckon? Morning, Jeff.'

Jeff tapped a weatherboard gently, searching for the stud. 'Morning, Molly.'

There was a bit more of that country stuff—how're the kids and how's the wife?—before it became clear that Jeff and his mate, Neil, had been hired to fix the leak and do some other repairs in the cottage. They'd begun work yesterday and already had the floors up in two rooms and were working on the roof.

'Real mess,' Jeff said. 'Like a lot of jobs, mostly fixing other peoples' . . . mistakes.'

I had the feeling that his language would have been saltier but for Molly. Jeff went on to say that they'd cleaned the cottage out and burned everything they found. Owner's orders.

'Good,' I said. 'I might want to rent it. That's why we're here, right Mr Jacobs?'

Horrie nodded. All the good mornings and other solicitations apparently constituted an introduction. 'Mind if we take a look around, Jeff?'

Jeff had no objection. We left him to the weatherboards and Molly to the paper, and went around to the back of the house. The yard was very long and the trees were as old as the building. Barbecue area, considerably over-grown; a flowerbed or two, likewise.

'Oscar wasn't much of a one for gardening,' Horrie said.

Nor for house-keeping, according to Neil. He was wrestling an electric stove away from the kitchen wall when we went in. He got it clear and rolled a thin cigarette from a packet of Drum, glad of the break.

'Bit of a shit-hole,' he said. 'Hasn't been cleaned in years. Mind you, not much cooking 'n' that went on. Bathroom's as clean as a whistle, but.'

There wasn't any point in looking through the house; the floorboards were up in the hall-way and two rooms and the place smelled of fresh sawdust and old damp. The bathroom was an outside building connected to the cottage by a galvanised iron roof. The bath was a big, old claw-footed job and the fittings were of similar vintage. Everything looked and smelled clean although a bit dusty. I wandered down to the end of the yard and confirmed the impression that to see the sea you'd have to climb one of the trees.

Walking back along Ocean Street, Horrie felt a need to justify himself. 'I tried to help him. Offered to lend him money to expand his busi-ness, suggested he put a deposit on a house. Could've helped him there, too. My bank thinks I'm the greatest thing since sliced bread. But he wouldn't be in it.'

'Very private sort of person, was he?'

'That's it exactly. I saw a fair bit of him.

Couple of times a week I suppose. We went fishing every other weekend. He was out of the area a few days a week doing jobs here and there. Up towards Cessnock, down to Lake Macquarie. All over the place. As I say, I never went past the kitchen in the house, but I knew it was no palace.'

There was some puzzlement in his voice and I pressed him. 'But you were surprised at how little he had, eh? How little business there was.'

'That's right. I should've helped him more.'

'Who owns the house, do you know?'

Horrie shook his head. 'Oscar paid the rent to an agent in town. Bit of a coincidence. Them getting to work on it just as you come up to take a look.'

I agreed that it was and we walked in silence back to his house. May was up and working in the garden. She and Horrie kissed affectionately and he told her about the renovation of the cottage. May sniffed, 'About time. That place was falling down. How are you feeling, Cliff?'

'Pretty good,' I said. 'Thank you for everything.'

She clicked her secateurs. 'For what? And now what are you going to do?'

'I'm going to show Cliff Oscar's stuff,' Horrie said.

She sniffed again and snipped through a rose stem. I followed Horrie into the house and through to a smallish room where there was a desk, a bookcase and several cardboard boxes and black plastic garbage bags. 'They call this the study,' Horrie said, 'but the only thing I ever

77

studied in here was the form guide. The stuff's in those boxes and bags. Take your time, Cliff. I'll go and see if I can get back in May's good books.'

'I'm not doing you much good there.'

He pulled up a blind to give me more light. The ocean looked to be only a few metres away, as if you could throw a stone into it. 'Can't be helped,' he said.

I lifted the plastic bags onto the desk and unwound their ties. I've sifted through the physical remains of a person's life a good many times and the feelings have always been the same—is this all you really had to leave behind? Is this the way you meant it to look? Why didn't you do something about that when you had the chance? The effects are always exactly what the word suggests—incomplete pieces, broken threads, interrupted business. It doesn't matter who it is—friend or enemy, lover or stranger—the feeling is of something left unsaid.

The effects of Oscar Bach triggered none of these sensations.

I went through it all very carefully—the business papers, documents, books and magazines. I lifted the tools and fishing gear and shaving kit out of the boxes and examined the clothes and shoes and fountain pen. There were no photographs, no pictures to hang on a wall, no personal letters, nothing old and useless, kept because it was loved. I remember telling Harry Tickener that there was a time when I could fit everything I owned into an FJ Holden. Harry said he'd once been able to fit everything into a

Volkswagen. Oscar Bach could've topped us both—the whole of his belongings would have fitted into a supermarket trolley.

Horrie Jacobs brought me in a cup of coffee. I remember thanking him but I couldn't remember drinking the stuff later. I was thrown into that state which is half cerebral, half instinctive. Bach's things had convinced me that he was truly a man of mystery. I was sure of only one thing—all these signs of the reclusive, anonymous bug sprayer and beach fisherman, did not point to the real man. He was someone else who did other things in other places.

There *had* to be a clue to the other man, but maybe it was in the cottage being gutted. Maybe I'd never find it. I went through all the stuff for a second time, as is my methodical way. I probed and rattled things and turned them upside down. An old leather jacket creaked and rustled as I felt in its torn pockets. I shook it and it rattled with more noise than the metal zip fastener should have made. I took the jacket across to the window for the light, turned it inside out and began to feel around the lining and stitching. There was something loose and metallic inside the lining near the waistband. I worked it around to a hole and poked it out. Two keys on a ring, one big and new, one small and old.

I put everything back the way I'd found it and took the keys and the empty coffee mug out to the kitchen. May was sitting at the table doing the cryptic crossword in the *Sydney*

79

Morning Herald. She looked up. 'What a beast to breathe on her,' she said.

'Sorry.'

'That's the clue—what a beast to breathe on her.'

I rinsed the mug and put it on the sink. 'How many letters?'

'Seven.'

'Panther,' I said.

She wrote it in. 'It fits. Do you do the crossword?'

'No. It was just a guess. Can you tell me where Horrie is?'

'He's in the garden. Did you find anything interesting in his things?'

There was something so direct and honest about her that I didn't consider lying. I noticed, though, that she didn't use Oscar Bach's name. I showed her the keys.

She shrugged. 'Horrie might know what they are.'

'Have you two made it up?'

'Nothing to make up. I'll love that man till the day they put me in the ground. I just wish he didn't have all this trouble.'

'I don't understand. What trouble? You're rich. He lost a friend but ... '

She put down her ballpoint and turned her dark, slanting eyes on me. 'You don't look stupid but you say some dumb things. Like all Australian men, you think women don't really know what's going on. I know, believe me, I know.'

'I'm sorry, May. You've lost me. What do you know?'

'I know who attacked you the other night, or who ordered it. Horrie doesn't know and you mustn't tell him. It would make him too unhappy. Go and talk to him, Cliff, but be careful.'

'What can you tell me about Oscar Bach?'

She shook her head and the fine, grey hair flew around her wise face. 'Nothing. But when you find out some more come and talk to me. Talk to me before you talk to Horrie.'

'What about Ralph?'

She picked up her pen and filled in an eight letter word.

9

I found Horrie weeding a garden bed. I'm no gardener, but the green things sticking up out of the ground looked like the tops of vegetables. He was on his hands and knees, bending forward and back easily. I wondered if I'd be able to move like that when I was his age. Maybe if I ate more vegetables? The sun was high and hot. Horrie wore a stylish wide-brimmed hat and, despite my thick head of hair, I felt the need for a hat, too. I showed him the keys.

'That looks like a key to Oscar's van,' he said, fingering the larger key. 'Don't recognise the other one.'

'There was no trunk in the house? Tool box, sea chest, nothing like that?'

'No.'

'What's this van? You didn't mention that before.'

'Must've forgot. Oscar had an old Bedford van for his work. Real wreck, but he kept it running. He must've been a pretty good mechanic. The young feller who's doing the work now's got it. Mark Roper. Leastways, he did have it a couple of weeks ago. I saw him in town. Said it was running all right. Is it important?'

I said I didn't know what was important yet, which was true. I got Roper's address in Lambton from him and told him I was off to pay a few visits.

He brushed dirt off his hands and stood up. 'You feeling all right? Need any help?'

I said I felt fine which was half-true and that I didn't need help. That disappointed him. He looked down at the garden bed as if he didn't care whether the things grew or not. It brought home to me again how important this matter was to him. I asked him to thank May for her hospitality and reassured him that I'd stay regularly in touch.

'If you need money . . . '

'I'll ask for it. Don't worry. No need yet.'

He took off his hat and wiped sweat from his forehead with his hand. 'Can you tell me this? Do you think I'm crazy or is there really some sort of mystery here?'

I still had a slight headache; I had a broken car window, a hostile son and a man who left fewer traces behind him than a bird flying across the sky. There's a mystery, Horrie,' I said.

Glenys Withers took one look at me and said, 'I knew you were trouble the minute I laid eyes on you.'

'That's not a very compassionate attitude,

Senior. I'm the innocent victim, not the vile perpetrator.'

'Attacked, were you? Did you report it to the police? I thought not.'

She took two steps down towards me, better than backing away, but I still felt I was losing ground. I'm no more of a fetishist than most men, but there was something about her strong, shapely body in the crisp uniform that was doing things to me. If I'd been forced to describe it, I'd have called it pre-sexual. First off, I wanted this good-looking woman to like me. Right then, I wasn't sure that she'd have a cup of coffee with me. I hadn't counted on kindliness. She stood a step above me which made her only a couple of inches shorter and looked at my face. 'My god,' she said, 'you have taken a battering over the years, haven't you? What happened to the nose?'

'Boxing,' I said, 'mostly.'

'That'd be right. What have you been doing, apart from being bashed?'

'Talking to Horrie Jacobs and looking through Oscar Bach's things.'

'Find anything interesting?'

I'd recovered my balance and had the half-truth ready. 'His old house's being renovated as of yesterday after years of neglect. Seems a bit coincidental. Did *you* find anything interesting?'

She touched my arm and shrugged her shoulder bag into place. The gun on her hip jumped a few inches. 'Come and have something to eat and we can talk about it.'

She took me to a semi-outdoors restaurant, part of the re-vamped waterfront. We sat under a pergola covered with a vine that grew out of a tub. It was that sort of a place—almost natural. She ordered a light beer and calamari and I opted for the same drink and whitebait. We made small talk over the beer while we waited for the food. I reflected that this semi-profession had changed: once, you had to be an ex-cop or something equally heavy and be ready to put in the boot, now, there's a TAFE course leading to qualification for a PEA licence and we lunch *al fresco* with gun-toting female cops.

She speared up some calamari, ate it and nodded. 'It can have the texture of a bicycle tube, ever found that?'

'Yes.' I crunched the bones and skin of some whitebait, chewed briefly and swallowed the lot. 'This is great.'

'Good, since it's all on you. The police force is feeling the pinch.'

I groaned at the joke and suddenly we were on better terms. She told me that Oscar Bach fell very definitely into the category of 'nothing known'. No convictions, no fines, no violations, no infringements, no complaints.

I said, 'Isn't that a bit unusual?'

She ate some of the side salad that had come without being ordered. It seemed to be fresh and crisp, but was it free? 'Yes, but not unique. In theory, all citizens should have a clean bill of health.'

'You'd be out of a job if they did.'

85

'So would you.'

'True. I have to tell you that I got the same result when I looked through his stuff. Too good to be true. No, worse than that.'

'What do you mean?'

'Not true at all.'

'You're being fanciful now. You're trying to promote something. That's the trouble with people in your business, always looking for angles.'

The tasty whitebait turned to ashes in my mouth. Suddenly I was angry. Where did she get off? Going from office to courthouse, attending the odd disaster ... 'That's your old man talking,' I said. 'How many private detectives have you dealt with, Senior? In your smooth ride towards the top?'

'What d'you mean by that?'

I started eating again and the food tasted better. I crunched the skin and bones, took a forkful of the salad and a solid swig of the light. I wished it was Newcastle Brown.

'You think I made this rank because of my father,' she snapped. 'I'm a better bloody police...'

It was getting out of hand. Her voice had risen and people were starting to look at us. I resisted the impulse to complete her sentence with 'person', and poured her some more beer. 'I'm sorry,' I said, 'we shouldn't be fighting.'

'Why are we, then?'

I looked at her over the plates and glasses and bowls. The light bouncing off the water made her eyes look even bluer than before.

86

You're not interested in blue eyes, I said to myself, *you like dark eyes. Think of Anne Bancroft*. But I liked what I was seeing much more than I wanted to. I tried to think of Helen Broadway. I needed help.

'What's wrong?' she said.

I shook my head and a laser of pain shot through my skull. I blessed it. Something to blame. I touched one of the cuts and winced. 'My head hurts. Crowbar.'

'Jesus. You should be in hospital or something.'

'I'll be all right. Not as young as I was. You don't bounce back from these things as quickly. We seem to have rubbed each other up the wrong way. I apologise. I need your help.' The words were not coming from the part of my brain that was thinking and feeling things.

She ate a little more calamari, drank some beer and lit a cigarette. 'D'you mind?'

'No,' I said, 'blow some over here.' Not much of a line but better than telling her to put it out. Maybe someone else would do that. It was a pretty clean-looking place and I didn't see any ashtrays.

'Let's get back on the point,' she said. 'Nothing known on Mr Bach. An autopsy was done, of course. If we find someone squashed flat with a refrigerator lying on top of him we still have to determine the cause of death.'

I nodded. Maybe tough talking was her way out of emotional confusion, the way excessive formality was mine.

'There is something slightly unusual about

87

the autopsy, but I wouldn't get excited about it if I was you.'

'What was unusual?'

'It was done here at the forensic unit of the Central Hospital, like most of them . . . '

'Most? Not all?'

'No. The workload must've got too heavy or something, because a couple of the bodies were shipped to Sydney. Mr Bach's autopsy was done here but the doctor who did it died of a heart attack himself a few weeks later. This was the only autopsy he did and, compared with the others, I'd have to say his report is perfunctory.'

'Can I see it?'

She opened her shoulder bag and took out some papers. She'd balanced the cigarette on the edge of a plate and it had burned away, forgotten. I resisted the impulse to reach over and stub it out before it burnt down to the filter. 'I couldn't photocopy reams of the stuff or someone might have asked me what I was doing. But here's a sample—a page of the Bach report and one of the others. And I still don't know why I'm doing this.'

'Your cigarette's going to smell of plastic soon,' I said. 'Can I see the papers, please?'

She dealt with the cigarette and I took the papers and it would have been hard to say whether she'd intended to surrender them or not. The waitress arrived just then asking if we wanted coffee. We both did. Another agreement, another diversion. I scanned the papers quickly. Dr . . . (signature scrawled in haste, indecipherable) had some talent as a writer. His notes on the injuries to his subject and their clinical consequences leading to death had a dramatic and convincing ring. Not so with the work of Dr Keifer McCausland, who wrote his name in a bold, round hand. It was all 'apparents' and 'evidents' and 'obviouslys'. Dr McCausland concluded that Oscar Bach had died from 'contusion and trauma' resulting from 'falling objects'.

The coffee arrived and we both took it black without sugar. I handed the papers back. 'I see your point,' I said, 'it looks a bit sloppy, but you couldn't promote anything on that basis.'

'Don't start,' she said. 'All you can take away from this is that you'd have had more confidence if Dr Thingummy had done the job. Right?'

'Right.'

'That's not much.'

'No.'

'Who bashed you?'

'I don't know for sure. Why're you interested?'

'You think I'm interested in you?'

'Again, I don't know. No reason to think so. Maybe you're tired of being in personnel and liaison or whatever. Maybe you want to do some policing.'

'You're right there. I do. Is there anything in this, really?'

'I'm sick of being asked the same thing. Another minute and you'll have me saying it's a clear case of suicide, just for the variation. I simply don't know, and I have to admit I'm a bit thrown. I'm not accustomed to dealing with policewomen.'

'What's the difference? You're lying to me just as you'd lie to a man.'

I sipped some of the thin, bitter coffee. 'That's not true. I mean, it's been known, but. . .'

'This is getting tricky,' she said. 'I assume you've got a few things to follow up?'

'One, at least.'

'Why don't you do that and get in touch with me again? I might have something more to add myself.'

That suited me. Her tone was neutral, not unfriendly. I fished out my Mastercard and waved it at the waitress. 'You wouldn't like to tell me what that something more might be?'

She smiled. 'I don't think so. Thank you for the lunch.'

10

In the old days if you booked into a motel, took off in the afternoon and didn't come back by midday, the manager would open up the room and start inventorying your belongings. Not any more. At the Hillside they held a signed credit card slip and they could play it any way they chose. The manager gave me a casual wave as I drove in and went back to supervising the cleaning of the pool. Good move.

I lay on the bed with my brain in neutral and only my digestion working. My head ached and I thought about taking some painkillers but fell asleep before I could translate the thought into action. It was late afternoon before I woke up and I tried to tell myself that an interview with the client, an investigation of the subject's possessions and a consultation with an officer of the law constituted a day's work and entitled me to an evening with *Lonesome Dove* and the TV. I failed to convince myself. I showered, cleaned up the cuts on my face, changed my shirt and headed for Lambton.

Lambton is to Newcastle what Erskineville is

91

to Sydney. Close in, old established, tradition-
ally working class and by-passed by the
trendies. I drove through the look-alike streets
until I located Yorkshire Road which must have
been named by someone stabbing a map of
England with a pin. There were no moors, no
pubs, no pits—nothing here for Freddy
Trueman. Mark Roper's place was a double-
fronted fibro bungalow—iron roof, chimney at
the side, garage at the rear—pretty much like
the one next to it and the one next to that. As I
got out of the car I was aware of two unrelated
thoughts in my head: I'd never gone calling on
a pest exterminator before, and I wondered
what Glenys Withers was doing just then.

I stepped over the low gate and walked up
the cracked cement path towards the front of
the house. Weeds sprouted through the cracks.
The porch was just a scrap of wood and fibro
tacked onto the front of the place—post-war
austerity. I went up the brick steps and the
porch boards sagged under my weight. They
also creaked loudly enough to make it
unnecessary to knock on the door. I did,
anyway, and it was opened by a tall, thin man
with shoulder-length dark hair. He looked to be
in his early twenties, wore a blue overall and
smelled of beer and tobacco. He was visibly
shaking which wouldn't have concerned me
overmuch except that he was holding a rifle and
pointing it at my navel.

'Are . . . are you Cliff Hardy?'

I had to consider this question. Maybe he'd
shoot if I said I was and I knew a rifle bullet

would travel faster over one and half metres than me.

I said, 'Are you Mark Roper?'

His nod seemed to accentuate his general shakiness. He didn't lower the weapon. He wasn't a bad-looking young man except for the close set of his eyes. I raised my hands in a parody of the 'hands up' movement. I thought he might follow my hands with the muzzle of the rifle. Worth a try, but he didn't do it. I took a step forward, putting me squarely within the doorframe. Sergeant O'Malley, my old army unarmed combat instructor would have been ashamed of me.

'Stop,' he said.

But he also moved back and O'Malley had taught me what to do when that happens. A backward moving person is halfway beaten. I twisted, came further forward, flattened myself against the wall and brought both hands down in hard-edged chops on the flexed bones and tendons of his forearms just above the wrists. He screamed with pain and dropped the rifle. I was ready for the movement and almost caught it cleanly. Bit of a fumble, but I got it on the half-volley and had the muzzle up under his chin before he could get any feeling back into his hands.

I pressed up into the tight skin of his jaw. 'Let's continue this discussion inside, Mr Roper,' I said. 'Anyone else around?'

He shook his head; the stretched skin scraped on the rifle muzzle and hurt him. Pain registered in his eyes and I believed him. He

93

backed away down the passage and I eased off with the rifle. It was .22 semi-automatic with the safety off. Fourteen shot magazine at a guess. Could do an awful lot of damage at close range. Roper knew it and as his chin came down and he looked into the business end of the barrel he shook so hard I thought his knees would buckle. I flipped the rifle up onto my shoulder.

'I'm not going to shoot you,' I said. 'Let's talk. Back here to the kitchen?'

He nodded and we moved down the passage, where damp had affected the pale green paint job, into the kind of chrome, laminex and lino kitchen I had had my first few thousand meals in. Except that my mum had kept the kitchen floor as clean as an operating table and this one was sticky with spilt food and drink. Roper slumped down into a chrome and plastic chair and I put the rifle in the corner by the sink and took up a position where I could stop him if he bolted for the door. But the confrontation had drained him and he didn't look as if he had any bolting in him. Making a cup of coffee might be his limit.

'Suppose you tell me what's the big idea,' I said. 'Do you usually meet people at the door with a rifle?'

He shook his head and reached into the pocket of his overall. He took out a packet of Marlboros and a lighter and got one lit. He drew the smoke in deeply and the shaking began to diminish. I passed him a saucer from the sink and he flicked ash into it. It had been a deep first draw.

'I know who you are,' he said. 'You're a detective from Sydney. Horrie Jacobs hired you because he thinks I killed Mr Bach.'

I did a quick mental resumé of the things that had happened so far. I couldn't place Mark Roper anywhere in the chain of information. With nowhere else to look for him, I asked myself if he could have been one of the kids in the Commodore at the level crossing and concluded that he wasn't. Too old. Wrong colouring. Puzzlement. 'Hold on,' I said. 'You're getting way ahead of me. You're right about who I am and who I'm working for. But where did you get this other idea?'

'I worked for Mr Bach. Now I've got his business. I'm the logical suspect, right?'

'Let me tell you something. There's no such thing as a logical suspect except in domestic killings. The logical suspect is the person who slept with the victim. Nine times out of ten that turns out to be the one who did it.'

He was most of the way through his Marlboro, listening hard. His skin was pale to the point of unhealthiness and he looked as if he had difficulty in maintaining an acceptable standard of grooming and hygiene. He made it, just, and I wondered about his domestic arrangements. The house bore all the traces of the parental home, gone to seed. Was Mark a loner, a middle-aged bachelor twenty years early, misfit and psychotic killer? Somehow, I couldn't see it.

He lit another cigarette and his voice was a thin, strained whisper. 'Are you saying I'm a homosexual? I'm not. I've got a girlfriend.'

I struggled to follow his logic, then I got it. 'No,' I said, 'I wasn't implying anything like that. I don't know anything about you, Mr Roper. And I don't know enough about Oscar Bach.'

He snorted through the smoke. '*He* wasn't a homo either, believe me, he wasn't.'

'What's that supposed to mean?'

He opened his mouth as if he was going to speak more than two sentences. Then he half shut it. 'I don't know,' he mumbled. 'Nothing.'

I was getting impatient with him. This man knew something I didn't and was being paid to find out. That cuts across kindness and compassion. 'Look, son,' I said, 'I don't give a shit how many girlfriends or boyfriends you've got. I want to know everything I can find out about Oscar Bach. You know something and you're going to tell me what.'

He glanced at the rifle. He was considerably closer to it than me but he made the right decision and looked away again. 'I can't,' he muttered.

'You don't have a choice. You pointed a rifle at me a while ago. I took it off you without doing you any harm but it doesn't have to stay that way.'

'You'd beat me up?'

I touched the wounds on my face. 'It's like this. I've come in for some rough treatment around here already. You can see that. My pride's been hurt and when that happens I'm likely to get impatient and take it out on someone else.'

He squashed out his cigarette and the face he turned up to me was twisted with misery. 'I'm not brave, you see. That's the trouble. They'll kill me if they find out.'

He'd at least given me a line of attack. 'Who's they?'

'Gina's brothers.'

'Who's Gina?'

'Gina Costi, she's my girlfriend—sort of.'

I'd had 'sort of' girlfriends myself, they're the worst kind. This young man had a bad case of the fear and confusions. I judged it was safe to take my eye half off him and I ran water into the kettle and set it on the stove. There was a jar of instant coffee on the sink and several dirty mugs. I rinsed two mugs, made the coffee and told him to get the milk. He obeyed automatically, like a compliant child. There was almost nothing else in the refrigerator apart from beer cans and a carton of milk. There was probably a packet of cereal somewhere, some bread and a jar of peanut butter. That'd take care of breakfast and lunch. It was odds on there'd be fast food containers in the rubbish bin. Dinner. He spooned sugar into his coffee and sipped it before lighting another cigarette.

'OK now?' I said.

'Yes.'

'Gina's brothers would kill you if they found out—what?'

He smoked and drank some more coffee

before replying. I took a sip myself. The milk had been just about to turn. I sipped again. It *had* turned. I put the mug down. Roper didn't seem to notice. He sucked down coffee and smoke as if they'd give him the courage he wanted. Maybe they did. When he'd almost finished the coffee he sniffed and said, 'They'd kill me if they found out that Oscar Bach raped Gina and I didn't do anything about it.'

11

Once he started talking it was easy to keep him at it. All he needed was a little prompting from time to time. He told me that he'd begun working for Oscar Bach on a casual basis about a year before. He didn't much care for his boss but he liked the work. To him, poking around under buildings was interesting. He was a bit of a snoop, he admitted, and also a hoarder. He found things—coins, tools, bits of machinery—and kept them. Sometimes he cleaned and mended these items and sold them.

'I made a bit of extra money that way.'

'Good for you,' I said. 'Go on.'

Gina Costi answered the telephone at Bach's house for a couple of hours each week and typed out his invoices. He handled all the money himself. It wasn't much of a job for Gina but she was an unqualified high school dropout and she was glad of it. Roper hinted that Gina didn't always use Bach's phone for business purposes. She called her friends, made enquiries for other jobs, tried to win prizes on the radio. Harmless stuff. Roper looked a bit shifty at this point. He was on his sixth or seventh cigarette and second cup of coffee.

'What else?' I said.

'Want a beer?'

'No. Go on. You'll feel better when you've said it all.'

'Well, that's how I met Gina. I used to go to Mr Bach's house sometimes to get the details on jobs and that? And she'd be there sometimes. Sometimes I went around to pick up chemicals and stuff.'

I was getting the picture. Sometimes they made love, on Oscar Bach's time and in his bed. I recalled the dark little cottage and thought how it must have been—hasty, furtive, afraid the phone would ring or Bach would return. Still, there was no telling. It might've been exciting. Roper seemed to think so. He butted a cigarette with new resolution and got up to open the fridge. I didn't try to stop him. There's a time in every story for beer and this was it. He took out two cans of Foster's and looked up at me enquiringly. I was still standing which seemed ridiculous now. He needed to talk. I nodded, took the can and sat down at the table. We popped the cans.

'I'll show you a picture of Gina.' He almost ran out of the kitchen into the next room and I could hear him opening and closing drawers. When he came back he handed me a large colour photograph, the kind they take in restaurants. It showed three people sitting around a table with wine bottles and glasses and plates—Roper, looking uncomfortable in shirt and tie, another dark young man with hooded, intense eyes and a teenage girl—fluffed up dark curly hair, round face, big eyes, as stupid looking as a sheep.

'Me and Gina and Ronny,' Roper said.

I nodded and returned the picture. 'You and Gina went to bed in Bach's house,' I said. 'One day he came came home and caught you.'

He had the can almost to his mouth. He was about to drink, wanted badly to drink, but he stopped. 'How d'you know?' The fear in his voice was like electronic distortion; the sounds trembled and warped. 'How d'you know?'

'Drink up, son,' I said. 'It's an old, old story. You're not the first young dickhead it's happened to and you won't be the last. Bach caught you. What happened then?'

Roper drank some beer and put the can down. It rattled as it touched the table. 'He . . . he said he would tell Gina's brothers unless she let him do it to her, too. He said he'd tell them he caught me raping her. But it was him! He raped her! She didn't want him to do it, she fought him. She hated it. I was so scared I just stood there.'

Foster's isn't my favourite beer and right then the mouthful I took didn't taste of anything. I swallowed it just to be doing something. Roper's head slumped forward and he banged it on the table three times, hard.

'I just stood there,' he sobbed. 'I just stood there.'

What was there to say? A hero would've stopped Bach, a villain would've helped him. Like

101

most of us, Mark Roper was something in between and paying the price for it. Guilt and remorse. Heroes and villains don't have to worry about either. I reached over and patted his heaving shoulders.

'Take it easy, son. Is the girl all right?'

His lowered head bobbed and he snuffled. 'Yes. But she doesn't see me anymore. And her brothers . . . '

'Tell me about them.'

He lifted his head and wiped his eyes on the sleeve of his overall. The close-set eyes made him look almost defective and the snuffling didn't help. I decided he was younger than I'd at first thought—nineteen, tops. He drank some beer and got another cigarette going. 'Gina's got three brothers, all older than her.'

'How old's she?'

He dragged in smoke and sniffed. "Bout sixteen.'

Great. Say he's stretching it by a year. That put her underage at the time he was screwing her. Still, this is the nineties. I said, 'Go on about the brothers.'

'Mario, Bruno and Ronny.'

'Ronny? The guy in the photo.'

'Yeah. Renato, but he's called Ronny. He's the youngest and the toughest. He's crazy. He's a bikie and if he found out . . . '

'Don't get into that again. They haven't found out so far, why should they now?'

'*You've* found out.'

'That's my job. What do these blokes do? Locals, are they?'

He nodded. 'Kahiba. Their father did real well around there after the war, bought a lot of land and built houses and stuff. Shops, you know. Mario had his own real estate business and Bruno works for his father. Ronny doesn't do anything much except bludge money off Mr Costi and scare people.'

I'd finished the beer and I took out my note-book and starting jotting down names just to give him some confidence. I got addresses for Mario and Bruno; Gina and Ronny lived at home, so I got an address for Costi senior as well. 'Why did you say Mario *had* his own business? What went wrong?'

'Nothing went wrong. He got hurt in the earthquake. They found him wandering around Hamilton. He got hit by a sign or something. He was in a coma for a long time. I think he still is. I'm not worried about him, or Bruno. Bruno's a bit of a wimp, just does what his father tells him. It's Ronny, really.'

He looked at me as if he was seeing me for the first time. Something like hope appeared in his puckered face. 'Maybe you could go and talk to Ronny. See if he knows anything. I'm scared stiff that he's just waiting for the right time to get me.'

I put the notebook away. 'I might have to talk to him. I can't tell yet. If I do, I'll let you know what I think.'

'You won't tell him, will you?'

'I can't see why I would.' I tried to say it as firmly as possible, but this was very shaky ground. I'd found out something about Oscar

103

Bach that my employer wouldn't want to hear. Always tricky. But Roper's statements would need corroboration and Gina Costi was the only other possible source. Even trickier. One thing I was sure of, Mark Roper was no kind of a suspect. I fished out the two keys I'd found in Bach's leather jacket and showed them to him. 'Recognise these?'

He fingered them briefly. 'That's the key to the van. Are you going to take it? Is Mr Jacobs going to stop me from . . . '

'Don't worry. Nothing like that. What about the small key? Ever see that before?'

Interest in something else than his own misery made him look less limited. He touched the small barrel key. 'Don't think so. But there's a sort of box in the van, like a trunk. It's locked. That's the sort of key that might fit it.'

I stood with only a slight creaking of bones. 'Let's take a look.'

I followed him out the back door and down some steps to a treeless yard that was half dirt and half grass. Nice things look nicer by moon-light, bad things look worse. This yard was a museum of things half-done or completed things half-decayed. The fences sagged, the grass was cut in spots and long and bushy in others; there had been an attempt to collect cardboard boxes, bottles and cans into one area but either animals had re-distributed them or the steam had gone out of the attempt.

'Looked better when Mum was alive,' Roper muttered as he led the way towards the garage. 'I haven't got much of a knack for house-

104

keeping. She always did everything.'

He opened the garage door, which sagged on its hinges, and turned on the light. An old red Bedford van stood on the oil and grease blackened cement floor. The garage was dark out of the immediate circle of the light but I got an impression of a tool bench, boxes, oil drums, bits and pieces. The place smelled of rust and neglect. No doubt it had looked better when Dad was alive. No fancy sliding side doors on the Bedford. Roper opened the swing-out back doors and climbed inside. He swore as he knocked his shin against something, then there was a scraping of metal on metal. He pushed a box about the size of an esky towards me. I got hold of it and lifted it clear, not hard because it only weighed about as much as a brick.

'You can put it on the bench,' Roper said, pointing, 'there's another light over there that Dad worked by.'

'Doing what?'

'I dunno. He just worked out here all the time.'

He switched on a bare bulb mounted on the wall above the bench. The Ropers hadn't gone in much for wattage. The box was metal, painted grey. In the dim light I couldn't see the keyhole. Youth has its uses—Roper turned the box and stuck a black-rimmed fingernail in the hole. I produced the key, put it in the lock and it turned smoothly.

'Always wondered what was in it,' Roper said as I lifted the lid.

'It's a credit to your honesty that you didn't take a jemmy to it.'

'Never thought of it, even.'

The first thing I felt in the box made me drop the lid and lock it.

'Hey,' Roper said. 'I wanna see.'

'Forget it. I'm taking this with me.'

'You can't do that. It's . . . I'm the . . . '

'You're not anything,' I said. 'Mr Jacobs is the de facto executor of Mr Bach's estate. I'm acting as his agent. I'm taking the box.'

He shrugged. His moods seemed to range all the way from despair to apathy. Mum and Dad had done a great job. I carried the box straight up to the street and put it in my car. Roper followed me, slouching, hands in pockets. He'd left his cigarettes in the house and I could tell he was twitching for one. I remembered the feeling. The sight of the smashed window seemed to put some life into him. 'What about me?' he said. 'You can't just go off.'

'You haven't done anything, have you?'

'No,' he groaned, 'that's the trouble.'

I got into the car and started the engine. He trotted around to stand by the window. 'I don't think you've got anything to worry about. If I have to make any use of what you've told me I'll make sure you're protected. Just carry on as normal.'

'Thanks a lot.'

My patience with him gave out. 'Stop feeling sorry for yourself,' I snapped. 'Clean your house and yourself up a bit and go out and find a new girlfriend. Thanks for the beer.'

I revved up and drove off leaving him standing under a street light looking like a shoeless orphan. *Hardy's therapy. Strong medicine. Good for what ails you. You're always bigger than your problems.* Not for the first time, I tried, automatically, to wind up the window before I remembered why it wouldn't wind. The night air was cool on my face, a little too cool. I felt in need of tender loving care and where was there to look for it? Those thoughts were too confusing. I fiddled with the winding knob as I drove and wondered if I could charge Horrie Jacobs for the damage. *That's better, Cliff,* I thought, *now you're thinking like a professional.* I stopped at a liquor barn on the way back to the hotel and bought a half bottle of Haig—one good professional thought deserves another.

What I'd found in Oscar Bach's locked box was a knife and it's a funny thing about knives—you can tell from the feel of them whether they've been used to chop up vegetables or clean fish or do something else. This is my gypsy grandmother in me talking, of course, but there's something in it. Back at the motel I poured myself a scotch and unlocked the box again.

By the time I'd laid everything out on the bed I was feeling sick. I'd had two solid scotches on an empty stomach, but that wasn't the reason. The box had held the knife, a ball-point hammer, some light rope, a pair of handcuffs, a clump of wadded tissues and an old leather razor strop. Inside a manilla envelope was a collection of newspaper clippings. These had been cut from several different papers; they were cropped and large sections of the reports had been blacked out with an oil pencil. What remained detailed the case of Werner Schmidt, thirty-seven, who'd been convicted of the abduction, sexual assault and malicious wounding of Greta Coleman, sixteen, of Heathcote. He'd picked up the girl on the Audley road, driven into the bush, threatened her with the knife, raped her and hit her twice on the head with a hammer. The prosecution alleged that only the arrival of a National Park ranger, who'd been surprised to see a car on the little-used fire trail, had saved Greta's life. As it was, she was permanently brain-damaged. The ranger had over-powered Schmidt and taken him to the police.

Schmidt had been sentenced to fifteen years imprisonment. Official documents, also in the envelope, showed that he'd served twelve years of the sentence, mostly at Parramatta. He'd been released four years ago, after opting to serve his full sentence, less remissions, rather than apply for parole. One of the cuttings carried a photo of Schmidt being escorted to court: round face, thin hair, burly build, could have been anyone.

The documentation was pretty worrying. But what really worried me was the knife, hammer and rope, the story about the rape of Gina Costi and a map with four crosses marked on it.

12

The map had been torn from a copy of *200 Kilometres Around Sydney* and the crosses were at Mittagong, Wentworth Falls, Richmond and Taree. I fingered the paper, trying to decide whether it was from a new edition of the guide book or an old. New, probably. The big question was whether the crosses represented actual victims, intended victims or something else? I eyed the scotch bottle, wanting another drink but knowing that, with nothing in my stomach, it'd set me on my ear. The answer wasn't in the bottle anyway. I put the stuff away, then locked the box and put it in the boot of the Falcon which I also locked. I put the distributor cap in my pocket and walked out of the motel court-yard towards a service station advertising just what I needed—'EATS'.

Over a greasy hamburger with chips and something pale green and pink they called a salad, I tried to work my way through the moral and professional thicket. If Bach/Schmidt, call him Bach, had still been alive, my duty would have been obvious—go straight to the cops because people are in danger. But Bach was dead and what I had was no more than evidence leading to the possible solution of possible crimes. Pretty thin. But there was more. If young women *had* been attacked or killed in those places, their families had a right to the information. I knew from experience that it's the silence, the never-knowing that eats the lives out of the parents and friends of missing kids. But if there had been no such crimes then the information I had was, strictly speaking, something that had been purchased by Horrie Jacobs. And it was the last thing he'd want to hear about his late friend.

I sat in the little cafe along with a couple of truckies who were complaining about the new speed restrictions and the drug testing. They agreed that the fun was going out of the work. One said he was thinking of selling his rig and buying a taxi. The other said he was thinking of going into the pleasure cruise business. Men on the move. They appeared to enjoy their food and the bitching, and they were in good spirits when they went back out to their trucks. I wondered if they were going to race each other to Sydney. I didn't taste the meal but I ate it for stomach lining and comfort. I had another problem with the contents of Bach's box. Did they give any clues as to who had killed him, if that's what had happened? Plenty to chew on.

There was a liquor store at the other end of the block and I bought a six-pack of light beer and a bottle of white wine, thinking that it was going to be a night that would need lubrication

110

rather than the wipe-out the scotch would provide. As I walked back to the motel I found
myself thinking about two women—Helen
Broadway and Glenys Withers. There were
good reasons for contacting both, quite apart
from the fact that I was alone in a country town
on a Wednesday night in spring.

I made instant coffee in the motel room and
wrote some notes on the day's work while I
drank it. That still left me with three hours
before I could go to bed and expect to sleep. I
could've read fifty pages of *Lonesome Dove* in
that time. I could turn on the TV and probably
get to sleep a little sooner, or abuse alcohol
with the same result. I cleaned my teeth,
poured a glass of wine and called the number I
had in my book for Broadway, Helen. My heart
was hammering in my chest as I punched the
last button.

'Hello. This is Michael Broadway. Can't come
to the phone just now. Please leave a message
after the tone. If you want Helen Broadway, her
number is Kempsey 56 0594. Thank you.'

More dialling. More heart hammering. More
wine.

'Helen Broadway.'

'Helen, it's Cliff.'

'Cliff. Jesus. Wait till I get a cigarette.'

I waited. Smoking more than her avowed two
a day, eh? Living apart from Michael. Strain in
her voice. And pleasure? Need?

'Cliff. Where are you?'

'Near Newcastle. I'm working for Horrie
Jacobs. You gave me a referral.'

111

'Oh, yes. That nice man. Good. That's good. God, it's amazing. I was just thinking about you.'

I didn't know what to say to that. Her tone was hard to judge over the phone. Not exactly cool, not exactly warm either. 'How've you been, Helen?'

'Lousy. Michael and I have split, finally. I suppose you gathered that from the answering machine? That's all I've spoken to for weeks—that bloody answering machine. Oh, well, it had to happen.'

'How's Very?'

'Not bad. She's old enough to cope. I've got a house in town. She floats between us.'

I remembered Verity, Very for short, as a lively kid. Bright, interested in a lot of things and happy with herself. Well equipped. I heard Helen expel a breath and I could see her with her Gaulois and the quizzical, amused expression on her face. Kempsey was, how far? I could probably get there if I sobered up and drove for a few hours. But we'd done all that, the midnight driving, the passionate arrivals and bitter departures. 'So,' I said, 'what brought this on? Did you . . . find someone else?'

Her laugh was throaty the way I remembered it, but harsh from smoking. 'Me? No. Michael did. A lady vigneron. She's installed out there now and I suppose they're lapping up a good red. Actually, she's a nice woman and I'm happy for him. She'll give him peace and be interested in what he does. Not like me. It's just a bit hard, being on your own after all those years.

Doing things solo. Including sex.'

That was Helen, direct and earthy. I could feel myself getting aroused—300 kilometres away and holding onto a telephone. What a world. I said something inane about marriage and asked her about her job at the radio station.

'Really good,' she said. 'I've got this morning program—guests, talk-back, raves. I love it.'

'I'll listen tomorrow.'

'You won't. You'll mean to, but you'll forget or be off chasing something or somebody. I wanted to do more work on Mr Jacobs' story but all this with Michael and Michelle blew up. Her name's Michelle, would you believe it? Jesus. Anyway, Mr Jacobs and all that . . . it just all got away from me.'

'I'm working on it. I wondered if you'd found out anything more.'

'No. Is that why you rang?'

'Yes. No, not really. I . . . I wanted to hear your voice . . . '

'My voice! Radio and twenty fags a day is ruining it. You sound a bit pissed. Are you?'

'Not really.'

'I know you. You've got a slight buzz on but it wouldn't stop you doing anything—go for a walk, read a book, go to bed. Shit, Cliff, I can't handle this. I'm hanging up.'

'Helen . . . '

'Don't say a thing. Not a fucking thing. I'll give you a call in Sydney or something, sometime. I don't know. 'Bye, Cliff.'

The cap had stayed on the scotch and the cork had gone in and out of the wine bottle only a few more times. I used the TV and good ol' Larry McMurtry to see me through the night. In the morning I ate the healthy parts of the motel breakfast and did my stuff in the newly cleaned pool. I felt fine. The cuts were healed, more or less, and my head no longer ached. After a shower and shampoo and shave, I checked myself out. Hair—dark, grey-grizzled; face—battered but holding together, two chipped teeth; some thin lines of fat around the mid-section, degenerated muscle; love handles, minimal. Could be worse. During my evening's light drinking and reading, I'd convinced myself that the separation of personal and professional life was alienating. At 10 a.m. I phoned Senior Sergeant Glenys Withers.

'Personnel. 'Sergeant Withers.'

'This is Cliff Hardy.'

'You're up and about early.' Ironical.

'That's me. I've found out some things about Oscar Bach that I think the police should know about.'

'Why are you talking to me, then? You want Chief Inspector . . . '

'No. Not yet at least. There's a snag or two.'

'There would be. Have you been getting yourself into trouble again? What is it this time? Broken leg?'

'Nothing like that. Were you serious when you said you wanted to move out of personnel, do some real police work?'

The flippant tone left her voice. 'Yes.'

'Something nasty has been going on. Rape for certain, murder possibly, but I haven't got very much at this point. I need to have your confidence and your help.'

'You've got a nerve. All I've seen from you is macho bullshit.'

'Come on.'

'All right, some rudimentary sense of professional ethics. Maybe. What is it now?'

'Do you have access to the computer records—unsolved crimes, MO breakdowns, case match-ups, all that?'

'Yes, within limits.'

'Could you find out whether there've been abductions, rapes, missing females, at Mittagong, Richmond, Wentworth Falls and Taree over the past couple of years?'

'Be precise. How long?'

'Four years.'

'I can give it a try. What else? I know there'll be more.'

'Run a check on Werner Schmidt, convicted of rape and abduction sixteen years ago.'

'Oscar Bach?'

'Looks like it.'

'It fits, I suppose. I've been doing a bit of work on him and he was coming up very dodgy.'

That was encouraging; the last time I had a cop doing work on one of my cases it was to try to get something on me. I hedged and backed off when she tried to get me to spill some more. No harm in trying, but I had to get before I could give.

115

'I'll be putting all this in my notebook,' she said.

'Only right and proper. Me, too.'

She gave me her address in Whitebridge and I agreed to meet her there at 6 p.m. That left me with eight hours to occupy. The day was perfect; bright sun with a little high cloud; a light wind to stir the trees and lift the waves. I promised myself a piece of it after I'd done something to earn it and used the phone energetically for half an hour. People splashed noisily in the pool, seizing the hour.

My calls to Sydney and then to Newcastle had put me in touch, through the journalists' circumlocutory network, with Barrett Breen, crime writer on the *Newcastle Herald*. We made the usual deal—I could scratch his back for information and he could scratch mine for a story if one materialised. I drove into the city and was inside Breen's cubicle in the busy office, shaking his hand, before eleven o'clock—there's something to be said for not living in the big smoke. Breen was a big man with the shoulders of a swimmer and the belly of beer drinker who doesn't swim much anymore. His grip was powerful.

'Mate of Harry Tickener's, eh?' he said. 'I've been meaning to write him a piece for ages. Some good stories up here.'

'You know Harry,' I said. 'He'll say it's shit, tell you to re-write it and say it's still shit. But he'll print it if it's any good.'

He was suddenly a bit less sure of himself and I got the feeling he didn't have stories to

116

burn. 'Mm. Well, I got those cuts for you. On the desk there. Good local angle to this?'

I nodded and sat down at the desk. Breen looked as if he hoped for more from me but I kept my head down and he made a quick phone call and left. Early lunch was my guess.

The abduction of Greta Coleman and the trial of Werner Schmidt had got more media coverage than usual because the girl's father was a prominent citizen—businessman and churchgoer—who'd called for the death penalty. The Wran government was in reformist mode at the time, emphasising the social context for crime, the need for counselling, rehabilitation. None of that was worth a rat's tail to Rory Coleman. He denounced the fifteen year sentence as 'weak-minded capitulation to the forces that are cancering our society'. Cancering, that was nice. He called for Schmidt to be executed along with all other such offenders. He had a fall-back position—if the weak-kneed, communist-leaning government wasn't prepared to put animals like Schmidt into the lime, it should at least have the courage to make them suffer physically. 'Werner Schmidt should receive one hundred lashes of the cat o'nine tails,' Mr Coleman was quoted as saying, 'and I would be happy to wield the whip myself.'

Coleman organised a 'fathers of rape victims committee'. It met in Heathcote and issued statements to the press. He turned up every day at the Glebe court where Schmidt was tried. At first he behaved circumspectly, but as the trial

117

went on, particularly when the defence intro-
duced medical evidence on Schmidt's mental
state, he became agitated, shouted and had to
be ejected. He created a major disturbance outside the court after the sentence was handed
down and narrowly missed being charged with
assaulting police and instigating a riot. He had a
lot of supporters.

This was the material that had been blacked
out in Oscar Bach's clippings. The cuts contained a few follow-up stories. One carried photographs of Greta before and after the assault.
She had been a pretty girl, blonde, carefree-
looking. The later picture showed a face from
which every trace of character and promise had
been wiped away. Rory Coleman hadn't shied
away from the camera; there were shots of him
holding placards, shaking his fist, looking dis-
traught. He was balding, wide-faced, belliger-
ent in expression and body language. If the
quotes were accurate, he was articulate, with a
good grasp of conservative arguments on the
issues of law and order and the punishment of
sexual offenders. He owned and operated a
number of carpet warehouses. He looked as if
he'd like to do his own TV ads, shouting abuse
at the opposition.

I read the clippings through carefully and
made photocopies of several, printing Breen's
name on the user list attached to the photocopier. I left a note of thanks on his desk and
one of my cards. My hands were dirty from
handling the distributor cap earlier and from
the newsprint, so the card wasn't the cleanest. I

hoped Barrett would be able to cope with that after lunch.

I bought a sandwich and an apple and some mineral water and drove to Redhead Beach. Kahiba was on the way and, just out of curiosity, I drove past the Costi house. It was set on a five-acre block, surrounded by forest; it looked like an old squatter's mansion restored to its former glory. Nice place—long verandahs all around, widow's walk on the upper storey, bay windows. There were several cars inside the gate, sitting around like discarded toys, and a big, black, stripped-down, high handlebarred motor bike. The Costi brothers sounded like an odd bunch—Mario, businessman and earthquake victim; Bruno, wimp; and Ronny.

The day had warmed up and people had taken advantage of it. There seemed to be more kids on the beach than was natural for a schoolday in October, but I suppose a lot of them could have had sore throats or upset stomachs. The older ones might have been in the study period running up to the HSC. If so, they were seeking inspiration in the natural world rather than in books.

I parked near the clubhouse which carried a sign saying that the Redhead Surf Livesaving Club dated from 1910. There was just one relic of that period around—a wooden lookout seat mounted on the rocks. Otherwise, the place was a model of the well-tended modern beach. The dunes were protected behind wire fences and were being re-grassed; there were plenty of litter bins and signs insisting on their use. The kiosk served food in paper bags and coffee in returnable mugs.

I changed in the shed and went onto the beach in shorts and T shirt feeling too old, too pale and too Sydney to really fit in. But once I was on the sand those feelings fell away. The sun was high and hot and the waves were curling and crashing about a hundred metres out. It would've been close on thirty years before that I'd surfed there. I remembered the massive, pink bluff that gives the place its name and the sweep of the sand all the way south for nine miles to the lake entrance.

Just like thirty years ago, it was swimmers to the left of the rocks, surfers to the right. No boogey boards then, plenty of them now. I joined the swimmers. The water was cold and clear. I waded out, slid under a wave and swam out to where they were breaking. The wind came back a few years after I stopped smoking, although the body strength has ebbed. I kicked hard in the old-fashioned way and chopped into the water, ducking under the waves that broke fiercely and threatened to push me back. I made it to the right spot with plenty of breath and strength to spare and noted where a small rip was running, off to the right. Be easier to get out in that next time.

After two misses, due to my bad timing, I caught the third one that came along, a high-curling, surging monster that broke behind me after I had some momentum up, collected me

120

and propelled me forward like a missile. I reared up, hunched my shoulders and saw the red bluff away to my left and the land, green and misty through the spray, and then I was locked into the world of blue and white water, jetting ahead with everything around me tight and controlled and beautiful.

I used the rip to get out and caught a few good waves, but none to equal that first one. I lay on the beach and ate the food and drank the mineral water. Although I didn't really want coffee, I had a cup just to support that sound environmental policy. A harsh Aussie voice over the PA system called for 'Wayne Lucas' and 'Adam Amato' and 'Brenda Kimonides' to call at the kiosk. I drifted off to sleep with *Lonesome Dove* as a pillow and the Falcon's distributor cap tucked away, dirtying my T shirt.

13

'Mister. Mister!'

The voice, young and piping, was close to my ear and a hand was shaking my shoulder. I looked up and was blinded by the low sun.

'You're going to get wet, Mister. Tide's coming in.'

My saviour was one of those truants, jiggers they call them now—aged about ten, skinny and brown, a true habitué of the beach. I thanked him and scrambled to my feet. Another minute or two and one of the more thrusting waves would've soaked me.

'Thanks, son.' I found a dollar in my shorts pocket and gave it to him. He looked at it doubtfully. I found a fifty cent piece and gave him that, too.

'Thanks, mate.' He ran towards the kiosk, flicking sand all over me with his take-off.

I collected my stuff and stood on the beach looking at the water. The surf was high and loud and the board riders were doing fine. Most of the swimmers had gone but there were still a few little kids playing on the rocks and bigger kids lounging around the surf club. Away to the south I could see people walking on the beach and a few immobile figures holding long rods and looking like permanent fixtures at the water's edge.

I was stiff from sleeping on the hard sand in an awkward position. A hot shower would have been good but the sheds didn't run to that. I stood under the cold water and rubbed and soaped and did knee bends until I felt loose. I hummed a few bars of 'The Sultans of Swing' and a teenager gave me a sideways look. I did a rapid calculation: he'd have been five or six when the song came out. I remembered my father crooning Bing Crosby numbers, off key, in the bathroom with the door open. I remembered the smile on his face and the pleasure he was getting. He must have been imagining himself in Manhattan, in a tux, with slicked-back hair and a willowy blonde waiting to dance with him. Instead, he had a semi in Maroubra and my ratbag mum, my sister and me. I went on humming defiantly until it was time to turn off the water.

It was too early to go calling on the Senior Sergeant but not too early to find out where she lived. Burwood Road branched off Dudley Road in Whitebridge. The houses were generally up-market and tasteless, colonnaded, triple-garage horrors, but hers was one of a set of four cottages facing the entrance to the Glenrock Nature reserve. The cottages were identical in structure but had undergone some changes over the years—bits added, verandahs closed in. My guess was that they were mine managers' houses, several notches up from the workers' houses. Glenys Withers' house was the last in the set, possibly the cheapest to buy, because it was in a dip and would not have had an ocean view. It was also the least adulterated.

I drove down the gravel track to Dudley Beach through light timber and scrub that didn't look to have changed since settlement. The ocean opened out in front of me after a particularly sharp and badly cambered turn and I almost missed the first stunning impact of the view as I fought the steering wheel for traction. The beach was long, wide and curving with rugged rock formations at either end. From this elevation and direction the water looked almost threatening, as if it would not be confined by the bay but would sweep up the sides and carve chunks out of the coast. Maybe it would. There was a car park at the bottom of the road, a rutted, half-hearted affair of posts and wire fences. It was a safe bet that not many of the BMWs and Volvos I'd seen in the Whitebridge driveways would risk their suspensions on the road or stand here in the blazing sun on a summer day. Dudley was still a beach for the people who went places on foot.

'Come in, Mr Hardy.'

She was wearing a black silk shirt and a blue and white horizontally striped skirt that came down well below her knees. Shoes with a bit of a heel. She had her hair pushed back from her face and held with some kind of a clip. Her forehead sloped back and her blue eyes seemed to bulge slightly. She smelled slightly of wine.

'Hello,' I said. 'Nice house. Best in the neighbourhood.'

She laughed and moved aside to let me into the hallway. 'Aren't they awful? And they keep getting worse. I'd had my eye on these houses for years and nearly went mad when they came up for auction.'

I had a folder under my arm which contained a selection of the Oscar Bach material. I'd hoped to impress her with it, but right now I was the one being impressed. The hall was painted in soft colours and the hardwood floor was highly polished. The place smelled of natural things—wood, earth and flowers. We went through to a sitting room-cum-kitchen that held a lot of light and just the right amount of furniture.

'White wine or beer?' she said.

'Wine, thanks.' I put the folder on the pine table and looked through the back window. The view was of open, lightly timbered country rising back up towards a ridge covered with the sorts of houses that decorated Burwood Road. She handed me a stemmed glass and followed my gaze.

'When I was little, all this was open way back up to the mine. These houses were all owned by BHP—leased to the the mine managers and engineers. They sold them off a year or so ago.'

125

'You were lucky some developer didn't buy them up and level them.'

She nodded. 'Lucky by six months. A bit earlier when the developers were flush, that's exactly what would've happened. As it was, the houses went to people who wanted to live in them. Sit down. Let's talk. What've you got?'

I sat and couldn't help laughing. 'You call that talking?'

She picked up the half-full wineglass that had been standing on the table and took a sip. 'I suppose not. We have to trade, do we?'

That had been my thought but now, looking at her, it didn't seem to make a lot of sense. The little bit of the house I'd seen spoke volumes— she lived alone, independently, made her own choices. Sleek brown hair and blue eyes, slim, shapely body below the slightly padded black silk shoulders. I was dry-mouthed and needed the wine. 'Glenys doesn't suit you,' I said.

'I'm called Glen, mostly.'

We stood simultaneously and I reached for her. Her body was strong and soft at the same time and she was taller than I'd thought. We came together at the thighs and I felt her arms go around my waist. I put my hand behind her head and searched for her mouth. We kissed like thirsty travellers finding a well in the desert. Her mouth was soft and it opened and we probed each other, taking something and seeking something more. When the kiss ended we were standing clamped together; I could feel her breasts against my chest and I put my hand up to touch them. She undid a button and

126

put my hand inside. She was naked under the blouse; my fingers closed over the soft, cool flesh and I felt her nipple rising.

Then her hand was over mine, holding it still, preventing further exploration. 'Are you married or living with someone?' she said.

'No.'

'That's good.'

Her bedroom was large and at the front of the house. I'd been right about the water view. From the window I got an impression of moonlight and stars, tree tops and clouds. I lay back with my head propped up on two or three pillows and didn't bother to try to make the images any clearer. Her head was on my chest and her hands were patting her groin. She was making little moaning noises.

'Good,' she said, 'that was so good.'

She was right. It *had* been good, tentative to begin with as we discovered what worked, what was exciting and unusual. We used our hands and mouths and I only entered her at the very end, almost as a courtesy that neither of us cared too much about. That, of course, made it all the more exciting and we finished by bucking and thrusting each other into sweaty exhaustion.

'It's only about eight o'clock,' she said. 'And we haven't eaten.'

'Hmm. I wouldn't say that.'

She laughed. 'D'you want to go out to eat, or something, Cliff?'

127

I kissed the top of her head. 'No. I'll eat anything you've got in the kitchen that isn't actually moving. I've had a very hard day—interviews, research, surfing, sleeping on the beach . . .'

'What beach?'

'Redhead. Why?'

'Nothing. I thought you might've gone to see Mr Jacobs with your information.'

'I can't do that until I talk to you.'

I felt her body stiffen slightly as some of the sexual languor departed. Well, it had to happen. I felt lazy and relaxed physically, but as I lay there and looked out at the night sky I was aware that this was only part of the story. I hadn't only come there to fuck. We seemed to reach similar states of mind simultaneously; she rolled away and reached for her shirt which was on the floor by the bed and I swung my legs clear and felt for my pants. We were holding up the garments, arranging them for putting on, when we both burst into laughter. We rolled on the bed, hugging and kissing and I felt the soft swell of her belly and the warmth between her legs.

'I'm too old,' I said.

'Don't be silly. Do the best you can. I don't mind.'

It was another half hour before we dressed and went back to the kitchen-dining room, both now seriously hungry and thirsty. Glen wasn't much into house-keeping. She had bread and cheese and eggs and a lettuce and tomatoes and onions and that was about all, apart from breakfast cereal and milk and some grapes. We boiled the eggs and laid the rest of it out, minus the cereal, on the table and ate it with a few glasses of the white wine to wash it down. I took the Bach file from the floor where it had fallen and showed it to her. It wasn't a time for negotiation—we were into the realm of trust or the past two hours had meant nothing at all.

She read through the papers as she ate and drank, diluting her wine with mineral water so that after the first two glasses it was scarcely alcoholic at all. I followed suit, heavier on the wine.

'How did you get on to this?' she said.

I told her about the interview with Mark Roper and the opening of Oscar Bach's box.

She examined the map with the crosses and pulled a face. 'You're hoping it's negative on these four places for rapes and abductions?'

I nodded.

'Don't know yet. The computer records aren't that good. I'd have to say it's maybe for Wentworth Falls at least.'

'What's the case?'

'Sixteen-year-old. Not the type to go missing, but vanished without a trace. Pretty blonde girl. Isn't it amazing? We fucked while we were holding on to this sort of information.'

I shrugged. 'They screwed in Belsen. Did you find out anything else about Schmidt?'

She tapped the photostats into a neat pile and slipped them back inside the manilla folder. 'Sort of. If anyone had bothered to look he would've shown up as very odd. His commercial references don't check out. He didn't register his business, didn't have any insurance. The name is a deed poll job, pretty recent. The driver's licence is an outright fake. He must have known somebody in that racket.'

'That figures,' I said. 'The question is, did he assault, rape or kill anyone in any of those four locations? If he did, you have to act on this, Glen.'

'I know. Get in touch with the detectives who worked on the cases, if there are any, contact the parents . . . shit! Well, that's my problem, but I can see yours—Mr Jacobs.'

'Right. He'll probably fire me. He won't want to hear any of this. Now that'll be OK by his son, Ralph . . .

'Who probably put the frighteners on you the other night.'

I looked at her, possibly with my mouth hanging open.

She reached over and touched the healed cuts on my face. 'We know about Ralph. He's a Sydney smoothie now, dead respectable, but not so long ago he was a real head-kicker. It wasn't too hard to figure out that he'd try to discourage you. Didn't work, did it?'

'No. I'd rather like to meet him again.'

'Again? So he warned you off?'

'The motto on my tombstone should read "he only had himself to blame".'

She digested that as we cleaned up the kitchen. She smoked a cigarette while she made coffee. She'd put on her silk shirt and her knickers but her legs were bare and I admired her slightly chunky calves as she moved. She caught me looking. 'Perv,' she said.

'You're safe for tonight.'

'You underestimate yourself, or me. Are you staying?'

'I don't know.'

'I'll come to your motel if you like. How's the bed?'

'I think it's got automatic massage.'

'Unnecessary. What's wrong?'

I would have been hard put to say. I liked her more than any woman I'd been with in years. The sex had been good and we were communicating well and building something, maybe. But I didn't know whether that was what I wanted. I could hear Helen Broadway's voice and the worst thing was, as I drank some wine and smelled Glen Withers on my fingers, the smell reminded me of Helen. There was no way to tell her this. I grinned and put the sheets back inside the manilla folder. My brain raced to find something to say to her that would explain my movements. 'Glen,' I said. 'All that checking and talking to detectives is going to take time. After tomorrow I probably won't have an employer but there's something I'd still want to do. You'll think it's crazy.'

She came across and gave me a kiss that tasted of salad and cigarette. 'No I won't. You want to go down to Heathcote and talk to Rory Coleman. I'd want to do the same. Just so long as you come back.'

14

I stayed the night. We made love again and slept and in the morning we walked down the gravel road to the beach which was clean and bright apart from a few things left on the sand by the tide. Glen walked along collecting plastic bottles and other rubbish and deposited it in the one bin on the beach. The bin was rusted and holey and the smaller bits of debris fell straight through onto the sand. I scraped them up and wrapped them in a plastic bag that had been half buried in the sand.

Glen shook her head. 'Animals. I saw a kid get off his board with a broken ankle strap. Would have been the easiest thing in the world to bring it up here, but he just tossed it on the sand. We don't deserve these beaches.'

'Looks like you do what you can,' I said.

'I have to go to work,' she said. 'You could get to Horrie Jacobs' place by foot from here if you wanted to. Just go to the end of the beach and you'll find a track. It'll bring you out down below his place. The walk'll do you good.'

She gave me a quick kiss and moved away. I

knew what she was doing—drawing some kind of a line under last night, avoiding goodbyes. I wasn't going away, just walking on the beach. She'd showed me where the key to her house was. I had her phone number. We were still co-operating as investigators. Anything else would develop, or not, according to whatever laws govern these things. As I walked towards the far end of the beach I felt something like the kids at Redhead—seizing the time. It was a good feeling.

There was less wind than yesterday and the promise of a warmer day, building on what had been left behind. The beach was wide and the grass and shrubs on the low dunes seemed to have a good purchase. There were shallow pools on the rock ledges and the couple of streams that ran down from the heights cut only shallow channels. Suede shoes and drill trousers weren't quite the right gear for beach walking and I was hot, with my shirt sticking to my back, by the time I found the path leading up through the timber. When it rained the track would be a watercourse but now it was just a rocky path, easy to negotiate, nicely shaded in spots, but steep. My breath was short when I made it to the top. I imagined little Horrie Jacobs bounding up it in his shorts and sneakers, and Oscar Bach . . .

I walked through the stretch of reserve to the bottom of Bombala Street and up the hill to the Jacobs' house. There was no-one in the shaded front yard, so I went up the steps onto the deck and around to the back of the house where the sun would reach. I found Horrie Jacobs sitting in a bright patch of sunlight at a wooden table with the newspaper and the remains of his breakfast in front of him.

'Cliff. Where the hell did you spring from?'

I told him I'd been talking to a police officer in Whitebridge, without giving him any of the intimate details. He poured me some coffee, then shook his head. 'It's cold. I'll make some more.'

'Don't bother. This'll be fine. I haven't got any good news for you, I'm afraid.'

'You believe Oscar was killed though. I can see it in your face. And you've got a policeman on side, haven't you?'

He was seeing something, but not what he thought. I nodded.

'But you don't know who did it?'

'There's a few candidates.'

He bristled. 'What does that mean?'

I told him, keeping it simple, not coming on too strong. I told him about Mark Roper and Gina Costi and about Greta Coleman and the prison term and the name change. I didn't tell him about the knife and the map. Something about the way he took the news, the way he drew himself up and sat rigidly, alerted May, who had been sitting inside the house with a view of the deck. She came out quietly and sat down next to Horrie. She heard some of it. Enough.

'I don't believe it,' he said.

'The evidence is all in my car. I can have it

here inside an hour. Senior Sergeant Withers can verify it all. I'm sorry.'

'He was my friend,' Horrie muttered. 'My only friend.'

May reached out and took his hand. He didn't resist, didn't seem to notice. The healthy colour had drained from his face and he looked old and frail. The woman looked at me and shook her head. I mouthed the words 'I'm sorry' again and she nodded and gave a slight shrug. A cloud moved across the sun and the deck was all at once in shade and cool. I shivered in my still damp shirt.

'You'd better go, Mr Hardy,' May said. 'I always knew that nothing good would come of this.'

I left them sitting there, close together, the man encased in misery and disbelief and the woman trying to communicate silently with him. She lifted her hand in what I thought was a small wave but she stroked his head. I dropped my own hand and felt like a doctor giving a patient the worst news possible. I slouched around the deck with my own distress building, wondering whether to get back to Whitebridge via the beach or the road. I stood in the carefully tended front garden, undecided, indifferent. I'd decided on the beach when I heard movement behind me. May Jacobs came down the steps from the deck and advanced towards me. She was wearing white track pants and a blue T shirt and she looked capable of jogging down to the beach and back up again.

'Cliff,' she said. 'That's a very unhappy man

you've made. Don't say you're sorry again. That's no good.'

'What *would* do any good, May? Just tell me.'

'Now you're planning to do what?'

'I didn't tell Horrie, but Bach *might* have attacked some other women. I'm working with the police on that. Horrie was right, you know. I think someone killed him and I want to know who.'

'Why?'

I shrugged. 'Just to complete things, I guess. A matter of professional pride. I ask a lot of questions and I like to get answers.'

'You make it sound like Trivial Pursuit.'

It was the first light note that had been struck since I arrived and it was welcome. I smiled. 'Something like that.'

'I love that man, Cliff. I can't stand to see him unhappy. There *is* something you can do. Find out all you can about who killed that man. Everything. Horrie Jacobs can face the facts. He spent his whole life doing it and he hasn't changed just because of the money.'

I nodded.

'He's worried that the money has changed him. It hasn't. I know. But he worries. Now this. It's better that he knows everything. Now it's me that's hiring you. You understand? I'll send you a cheque.'

I started to protest but she cut me off with an angry gesture. 'Find out! And tell us.'

She turned and marched away. I changed my mind and decided to go the road route. The sun came out from behind the cloud and I felt quite a lot better.

The walk to Whitebridge took about half an hour. Near the football ground, flanked by the two pubs, I saw a sign which warned of 'burning chitter'. I'd seen similar signs on the south coast and it indicated that the oval had once been the pit head. There was probably a shaft under it heading straight out to sea or back under Ocean Street, or both. That also explained the two pubs—an early and a late opener to cater for the mine shifts. I bought a paper in Dudley and glanced through it as I passed the school and the Post Office. Ailing economy, political manoeuvring at home, trouble abroad—nothing new.

Glen had taken Oscar Bach's box and the evidence it contained as I'd said she could. I was left with my file and photocopies of some of the the notes she'd made on her own Bach researches. I had a shower, drank a can of beer from her fridge and left her a note that said a whole lot or nothing, depending on how you looked at it. Being a snoop, I wandered through the house, snooping. It was a very plain place, solid, with what the agents would call 'tons of potential'. The trouble is, you need money to realise the potential and Glen didn't seem to have it. The renovations—a larger deck, bigger windows—had been done on the cheap and the lino tile laying and most of the painting had been done by an amateur. She had a few nice pictures on the walls and a family photograph on top of a bookshelf stuffed full of paperbacks, including *Lonesome Dove*. The picture showed a good-looking woman and the not so good looking Edward Withers with a boy and a girl who could only have been Glen and her brother. Wholesome stuff.

I put the key where it went and drove back to my motel to shave, pack and check out. The cleaner wouldn't have much of a job to do there. The sun was high and bright and I was sorry to be leaving Newcastle. I tried to enjoy the views as much as was consistent with careful driving. Along the road there were several blocks of land for sale. Two carried Mario Costi Real Estate signs, but they also had fresher signs from other agents. I wondered who was running Mario's business now. Maybe Bruno. Certainly not Ronny.

I was almost to Belmont before I noticed the dark grey Toyota. It stayed well behind in the thin traffic and I couldn't get a look at the driver. I considered trying some tactic to intercept it but nothing suggested itself. If I stopped it could pass and pick me up somewhere else. Presumably the driver knew the road patterns. I shrugged and let the car follow me all the way to the Swansea Bridge. It peeled off once we'd crossed the water and I felt like an outlaw being escorted across the county line. I made a mental note to ask May to call Ralphie off.

15

I made Glebe in under two hours which was good going for a couple of well-worn vehicles like the Falcon and me. The cat is well-worn too, and he can survive my absence for anything up to a week. The first couple of days he doesn't even notice and he was casual about the food and milk I put down for him.

'Screw you,' I said and he yawned, lapped up some milk and went off to lie in the sun on the bricks that Hilde had laid, beside the rubber tree Helen had installed. *Dangerous memories, Cliff*, I thought. *You're about as much use to a woman as a crack in a glass eye*. I used the beeper to get the messages on the office answering machine and learned nothing worth knowing. Then to the detective's secret weapon—the telephone directory. Rory Coleman still operated in the southern suburbs. He had a home address in Engadine and his showroom—there seemed to be only one now, but big—was on the Princes Highway at Heathcote. It was early afternoon on a bright, sunny Friday. Where would an aggressive marketeer like Rory be? In a meeting? On the golf course? In the showroom? My information was sixteen years out of date but I bet on the showroom.

'Coleman Carpeting. Can I help you?' Carpeting? She sounded as if she'd stepped out of a Woody Allen movie.

'Mr Rory Coleman, please.'

'May I have your name, please?'

'My name is Cliff Hardy. I want to speak to Mr Coleman about Werner Schmidt. Let me spell it for you, That's W-e-r-n-e-r S-c-h-m-i-d-t.'

'Thank you. Mr Hardy. I'm putting you on hold.'

A Christian-message radio station came on—unctuous announcer, a Biblical text and then a band called U2 which seemed to make just as much noise and little sense as the rest of them. My accountant's hold-music plays Mark Knopfler. I suddenly felt warm towards my accountant. I shook my head in disbelief. It was going on for two p.m. and I hadn't had a drink. That must be the trouble. The music stopped and a smooth, salesman's voice came over the line.

'Rory Coleman.'

'My name is Cliff Hardy, Mr Coleman. I'm a private investigator.'

'Yes? You mentioned Schmidt?'

How to play it? If he'd killed Schmidt and he thought I knew, what would he respond to? And if he hadn't killed him . . . ? 'I think we should have a talk, Mr Coleman.'

'Do you now? I take it you're from the Wilson agency?'

I was confused. Carl Wilson ran a detective agency, not a very good one. I'd have mended cat tyres before working for Wilson. 'No,' I said. 'No connection.'

'I have an arrangement with Mr Wilson. He is to convey any information about Werner Schmidt that may arise to me. I was hoping you were calling to tell me that Schmidt had terminal cancer. I'm sorry, that's not a Christian thought.'

'No, but don't feel bad. He's dead, Mr Coleman. I think we should meet.'

This is dumb, I thought, *he jumps in his Mercedes and off he goes*.

Coleman threw me completely. 'Lord,' he said. 'I thank you for the answer to this, my prayer. Let me feel compassion and something of your own mercy and not merely hate. Lord. I thank you.'

I said nothing.

'Mr . . . Hardy. I want to hear what you have to say. Can you come to my house in Engadine? Say in two hours?'

What else could I say? 'Yes.'

'Bless you, Mr Hardy.'

Oppenheimer Street wound around the northern edge of Engadine. As in most streets in suburbs where the residents are proud of their native gardens, house numbers were hard to find. These people don't want to paint numbers

141

on the trunks of their Illawarra flame trees and the banksias and other stuff obscure the fences and gateposts. But I found it eventually by trial and error—a large, rambling, ranch-style house with a bit more of the flame trees and banksias and everything else than the houses nearby. It also had a high security fence and gates that looked as if you didn't just lift the catch and walk in. I parked in the street, which left me a deep ditch and a wide nature-strip to cross before getting to the gate.

There was a squawk box on the gate. I pressed the button and stated my name and business the way the recorded message asked me to. A buzzer sounded, and a smaller gate beside the one that would have let in a coal truck slid open. I went through and up a bricked driveway. Beyond the house I could see deep green slopes that suggested forest and water. I recalled the map in the street directory and figured out that the Woronora river must be just across the way. That put Rory Coleman's house about as physically close as it was possible for a private citizen to get to the Lucas Heights nuclear reactor. Suddenly, the timbered slopes didn't look so inviting.

There was nothing special about the house— a million or so dollars buys pretty much the same thing anywhere—plenty of wood and glass, width and depth to all spaces, soft, springy stuff underfoot. A man met me at the door and would have taken my hat if I'd had one. As it was he simply led me down a number of corridors and ushered me into a room which was in the east or west wing of the house—I'd become disoriented. The room had a glass wall that looked directly out towards the Atomic Energy Commission establishment. A man was standing with his back to the door. He turned around as he heard his servant cough.

'Mr Hardy. Good of you to come. What do you think of the view?'

I was too busy taking him in to spare much for the view. Since his placard-holding, street-fighting days, Rory Coleman had put on a lot of flesh. It would bulge if he gained any more, but for now it was packed pretty tightly on his tall, wide frame. He was an inch or so taller than me, about five years older and twenty times more prosperous. I walked across the white wool rug spread over the polished board floor and shook the hand he held out. He immediately placed his other hand on top of our joined fists and I equally immediately took a strong dislike to him. He was wearing a white shirt, dark tie, grey trousers and glistening black oxfords, none of which helped to correct my first impression.

'Thank you for seeing me so promptly, Mr Coleman.'

'The view, Mr Hardy. The view.'

I looked through the glass at the complex which was more or less visible through the trees. Roofs, windows, chimneys, antennae, wires, and the huge white concrete sail-shape dominating everything. I preferred the trees. 'Impressive,' I said.

He released my hand. 'It is indeed. Nuclear

power represents the future. I'm a great believer in the future. I built this house as close as possible to the reactor to demonstrate my faith in the future.'

I nodded. It wasn't a promising start, given that I'd come to talk about the past.

'Can I get you something—tea, coffee?'

'Coffee would be good, thanks.' The servant was still at the door. Coleman said, 'Coffee for Mr Hardy please, Richard.'

Richard sloped off and Coleman indicated that I should sit in one of the three leather armchairs. I took one facing away from the future, enabling him to sit opposite it and make sure it didn't go away, if that's what he wanted to do. It seemed so. He sat quietly looking out the window until Richard came back with a coffee pot and other things on a tray. He got a small table from somewhere in the room and put it by my chair. He left me to pour the coffee—a nice, manly touch.

'It's over sixteen years since my daughter was attacked,' Coleman said abruptly.

'Yes.'

'I take it you're familiar with the details of the case, Mr Hardy.'

'Yes. And with your behaviour at the trial and subsequently.'

'Ah, yes. All that. It seems to have happened in another life. In a way it did.'

I poured some coffee and took a sip. It was thin and weak. 'What do you mean?'

'Are you a Christian?'

'No.'

144

'I thought not. You have a hardness about you. An unforgiving quality.'

'Did you forgive Werner Schmidt?'

'In time, Mr Hardy, I did. I found Jesus and he helped me to forgive. You tell me Schmidt is dead?'

I put the cup down. Some of the coffee slopped into the saucer and onto the top of the stool. Another big job for Richard. 'Yes. It looks as if he was murdered.'

'Ah, I see. And you've come into my house to meet me and decide whether I murdered him.'

'Or had it done.'

'Yes. That happens, doesn't it?'

'In the best of circles. The person I'm working for doesn't move in the best of circles but she wants to know who killed Schmidt. It's important to her.'

'Why?'

'It'd take too long to explain. I doubt that there's much I could do if you *had* paid for the murder.' I waved my hand at the window and the furniture. 'You seem to have the resources. Unless you were very careless you shouldn't have any problems. Still, no harm in asking. Do you remember the Newcastle earthquake?'

'Of course.'

'Where were you when it happened?'

'In my showroom. We felt it quite strongly. Some of the stock was displaced.'

'Any witnesses?'

'Certainly. About twenty or so of my staff. Are you telling me Werner Schmidt was killed in

145

the earthquake? That can't be. I read the names in the newspaper . . . '

'People change their names, Mr Coleman. Schmidt was going under another name and he died on the day of the quake. Whether it killed him or not is another question.'

'Remarkable.'

I expected him to say something like God moves in strange ways, but he didn't. He was an actor and poseur from way back. Now he sat with his chin resting in his plump, white hand. He wore a couple of gold rings, one with a large black stone in it. He was playing the thoughtful being, the philosopher. Could this softie, this born-again moneymaker, have ordered a hit? He was too armoured in righteousness and self-approval to judge. I took another sip of the lousy coffee and said, 'How's your daughter these days, Mr Coleman?'

It was a brutal, full-frontal thing to say, but I had to do something to shake that smug composure. His chin slid away from his hand as if he'd been left-hooked by Dempsey. His big, meaty shoulders convulsed; wrinkles bunched around his eyes, and from plump and rosy he changed to pale and flabby in a matter of seconds. The composure shook but did not break. I watched, feeling guilty but fascinated as he put the whole thing back together again. He drew in a gasping breath, touched one of his rings, smoothed his hair and let the hand drift down to tug at an earlobe. The smile came then, slowly but with close to full candlepower and the lines and wrinkles on his face were smoothed out. 'She is in very good hands, Mr Hardy. She is not unhappy. How many people can say the same? Can you?'

Good question. I stared at him as he completed the transformation back from stricken parent to grateful believer. I decided he was genuine, in his own terms. He wouldn't kill anyone, he didn't need to. God and good accounting would provide. I muttered something about needing to be sure and he nodded sagely.

'I remember what the vengeful impulses felt like,' he said. 'I wanted to kill Werner Schmidt and I would have, if I'd been given the chance. Thank the lord it didn't come to that.'

'I've seen the press photos,' I said. He smiled again, more genuinely still. 'I almost went to gaol. I've had something to do with prisoners since and I wish I had had that experience. It would have helped my empathy, perhaps.'

This was getting too rich. 'I doubt it,' I said. 'I've had a touch of gaol and all it gives you is constipation, indigestion and boredom.'

'I suppose it depends how you spend the time. You must be wondering, Mr Hardy, why I asked you here when we could virtually have conducted our business on the phone.'

I shrugged. 'I would have wanted to meet you anyway. But ... what's your point, Mr Coleman?'

'You say you have a client for this enquiry of yours?'

'That's right.'

'Can you accept two clients on the one matter?'

'It's unorthodox, but it's been known to happen. Why?'

'You've sized me up and you don't like me. I can accept that. I've also sized you up and, while I have many reservations about you, I don't think you are a mindless thug like many members of your profession.'

'Thank you.'

'Mr Hardy, there's someone I think you should meet.'

16

Richard was waiting outside a side entrance to the house, putting the finishing touches to the polish on a white Mercedes. I wondered whether owning a Merc was another sign of faith in the future. Probably. Coleman and I got in the back and I settled into a leather seat that felt as if it had been hand-built, specially for me.

Coleman said, 'Mr Fanfani's place, please, Richard.'

'Sir.' Richard put the Merc into drive and we slid forward without feeling anything so vulgar as the turning of wheels. Richard used a remote control device to open the gates and we cruised out onto Oppenheimer Street with scarcely a pause.

The car wasn't quite a limousine—there was no bar, TV or stereo—but it was opulent enough. Coleman gazed out of the window at the houses where, in all likelihood, some of his carpets were laid. I was still feeling some contrition about the way I'd hit Coleman with the question about Greta. The feeling had made me compliant, up to a point, but now I was getting impatient. 'This is impressive. I like the feel of a good car. But would you mind telling me where we're going?'

'To see a man named Antonio Fanfani. He lives in Loftus, not far away.'

'I didn't think anyone lived in Loftus.'

'I sometimes think that people like yourself, who work and live in places like Darlinghurst and Glebe, are a different species from us suburbanites. What do you think?'

'I think you've done some checking up on me.'

'Yes. And I telephoned Mr Fanfani as soon as I finished talking to you.'

'Who is he? What's he got to do with this?'

'I believe in letting people speak for themselves. You had your say and I had mine. We should let Antonio do the same. I will tell you this—he was a member of that organisation I formed.'

'The fathers of rape victims thing?'

'Yes. That was very ill-advised. It bred distress rather than comfort.'

We were going north-east, on the Princes Highway, with the National Park to our right. 'I don't know,' I said, 'sounds pretty natural to me. If I had a daughter and she got raped I'd want to do some damage to the rapist.'

Coleman nodded. 'Of course. That's a phase of the reaction. But you can't do that damage without damaging yourself and others who depend on you. You have to find some other way of coping with those feelings.'

150

'God?'

'For me and my wife, yes. Not for Antonio Fanfani, unhappily.'

Nothing more was said on the drive. The Mercedes pulled up outside a big house with a three-car garage, white pillars and lots of white plaster work around the top floor balcony. It looked like the sort of house put up by people who've spent most of their time living in two rooms. The concrete drive was wider than it needed to be, the lawn smoother, the front gate higher. There was a fountain in the centre of the front lawn with a small religious shrine built into it.

'Mr Fanfani's a building contractor,' Coleman said. 'That's how we became acquainted. He was a very good customer of mine, still is.'

We got out of the car. Coleman gave Richard a few errands to perform and the Mercedes purred away. We went through the open gates. There was a small car and a boat in the garage, plenty of room left for a Merc. 'I thought builders were feeling the pinch,' I said.

We walked on a series of concrete circles set in a meandering pattern in the smooth lawn towards the tiled, colonnaded porch. 'It's a matter of strategy,' Coleman said. 'If your business is dependent on the vulnerable part of the system you'll feel the pinch, as you put it. If not, not.'

'How're you fixed?'

He smiled as he pushed the bell. 'Most of my business is with the government and its agencies. Also with banks and insurance companies and big contractors who deal similarly.'

Chimes sounded inside the house and a stout, middle-aged woman answered the door. She beamed when she saw Coleman and the two exchanged a quick hug.

'Rory, so good to see you.' Her English was heavily Italian-accented.

'Hello, Anna. God bless you. How are you?'

'Not bad. Is this the man?'

Coleman stood aside. I felt I should bow, but I contented myself with getting through the door onto the white shagpile carpet and doing a little head-bobbing. 'Mrs Fanfani.'

'This is Mr Clifford Hardy. He's a private investigator,' Coleman said.

Her heavily-ringed hands flew up towards her face. She was a handsome woman in a fleshy, conventional way. 'Oh, Tony wants to see him so much, I know. He's in . . . that room, Rory. You know the way. I'll bring coffee into the den, or perhaps Mr Hardy would like something else?'

Coleman had arranged his face in what I took to be teetotal lines; I was tired of playing by his rules. 'I'd like some beer, Mrs Fanfani, if you have it.'

'Foster's or Resch's?'

Someone in the family didn't spend all their time praying and being polite. 'Resch's, thank you.'

Coleman led me through glass doors that opened onto a vast living room and down a passage to a part of the house where everything seemed to be on a smaller scale. He knocked on a plain door and a voice behind it said, '*Sì*.'

We went into a cell. The room was tiny—grey painted walls, small window set high up, cement slab floor, camp bed along one wall and three wooden chairs opposite. A man was sitting on one of the chairs. He was cadaverous—dark, folded in on himself. Not old, not young. His skin was olive but unhealthy looking as if it had been deprived of the sunlight it needed. His white hair was thin. He didn't get up. His hand, a claw coming out of a white cuff under a dark suit jacket indicated that we should sit on the chairs.

'Antonio,' Coleman said. 'This is Mr Hardy.'

Fanfani nodded at me. 'I'm very pleased to meet you.' He had only a slight accent, more a hesitation before certain sounds.

'Thank you.' I didn't sit down. I wasn't going to stay in that room one second longer than I had to.

'Anna's bringing coffee to the den,' Coleman said.

Fanfani nodded. 'I just wanted you to see this place, Mr Hardy. Before we spoke. This is where I do penance for causing my daughter's death.'

There wasn't much to say to that. As a place for doing penance, it looked about right. It was the sort of room in which a smile would be out of place and a laugh unthinkable. We trooped out and up a flight of stairs and along to a room with armchairs, a writing table and a couple of filing cabinets in it. There were several photographs on the walls and I was careful not to look at them, not yet. Curtains drawn across the window kept the light down and if you wanted to call it a den you could. But there was none of that cosiness you associate with the word. It came to me then—everything and everybody I'd seen so far in this house carried an air of sadness.

Mrs Fanfani arrived with coffee and an ice bucket that held two cans of Reschs pilsener. She handed me a can and a frosted glass. We got the pouring and stirring and can opening over and settled back in our chairs. All except Mrs F., so far the least gloomy member of the party. She went out after squeezing her husband's hand.

'I had a daughter, Mr Hardy,' Fanfani said. 'Angela. Her picture is on the wall there.'

I looked at the family portrait. It showed a younger Antonio with more and darker hair, a slimmer Mrs Fanfani and a pretty, dark-eyed girl in her early teens. The affection between them was palpable, even in the posed, tinted studio portrait. It was obvious in the way they sat and the inclination of their heads.

'She disappeared sixteen years ago. She would be twenty-nine if she were alive today.'

He was talking about big stretches of time but his grief was mint fresh. I'd seen it plenty of times before—the anguish of parents who'd lost, or feared they'd lost, children. Exposure to it may be one of the reasons why I've never risked having children myself. There's no other grief quite like it, and nothing like the relief of finding that it isn't so. Some people can bounce back from it surprisingly quickly, others never do. Antonio Fanfani was in the latter category. There was plenty of force left in him, possibly even ruthlessness, but something vital had been cut away. I sat quietly, drinking the icy cold beer, and wondered why Coleman had brought me here. Was he proposing Fanfani as Schmidt/Bach's killer? Somehow, I didn't think so.

'I believe that the man who abducted and raped Rory's daughter was also responsible for the murder of Angela,' Fanfani said slowly. 'I tried to persuade the police of this. Tried to get them to talk to . . . Schmidt about it. But . . . ' he opened his hands in a gesture of helplessness.

'The lawyers prevented this line of enquiry,' Coleman said. 'Completely cut it off. The prosecution agreed; it had a watertight case. It didn't want any complications.'

I didn't really want to know. I didn't want to get in touch with the kind of pain that would cause a man like Fanfani to suffer for sixteen years, to have a mortification room in his house. I suspected that the fountain shrine was part of the same syndrome. My rational, atheistic spirit rebelled against it all. But I had Horrie and May Jacobs to consider. Professionalism. Connections. 'Why do you suspect Schmidt was responsible, Mr Fanfani?' I said. 'Do you have any evidence?'

'What did the lawyer call it, Rory? The one I talked to a hundred times?'

'Circumstantial,' Coleman said. 'Angela was last seen on the Audley Road a few weeks

155

before Greta was attacked. She had had an argument with Antonio . . . '

'About sex,' Fanfani exploded. 'About boys and sex. My god, I wish she had taken a dozen lovers, a hundred. I . . . ' He buried his face in his hands and wept.

Coleman patted Fanfani's bowed shoulders and went on talking, the man who had come through, who had understood. I felt some respect for him, but still no liking. He told me that Angela Fanfani had admitted to having sex with a boy at her school. Her father had found the contraceptive pills and he had shouted and struck her. 'They are good Catholics,' Coleman said. 'You can imagine the scene.'

I could. I sympathised—with everyone involved, but I was still searching for the connection. Fanfani seemed to sense my puzzlement. He pulled himself together and drank some coffee. His pale claw of a hand brushed tears from his face. I took the opportunity to pop the second can of beer.

'I joined Rory's organisation and was one of its most passionate members,' Fanfani said. 'I was arrested several times. I was obsessed. I demonstrated at other rapists' trials. I, what is the word? Lobbied, yes, lobbied, the ministers for stricter penalties for the rapists and murderers of women and girls. I was mad for many years, wasn't I, Rory?'

'Possessed, perhaps,' Coleman murmured.

I drank some beer. *Am I in weirdo territory here?* I thought. *Are we going on to seances and ouija boards?* But Fanfani's behaviour was

156

acting against this doubt. He sipped some more coffee, blinked his eyes clear and seemed to be pulling himself up to some plane of rationality and strength.

'Mr Hardy,' he said. 'I gave up the idea of revenge for the loss of Angela. I still grieve for her and I still blame myself, most definitely. You have seen the room where I do penance.'

I nodded.

'Rory was a great strength to me, us, through all this. He helped me, more than the priests, to understand that god has a purpose although we don't always know what it is. He helped me to go on.'

Worth thousands of yards of burgundy Axminster, that, I thought. I didn't say anything.

'Eventually, I gave up my wish for revenge. I admit I had spent hundreds of hours thinking about how to kidnap Werner Schmidt and, god forgive me, torture him into admitting what he had done. I would then have killed him most cruelly, slowly . . . '

'Antonio,' Coleman said.

'I am sorry, my friend. My wife and I have no other children, Mr Hardy. Just Angela.'

I looked at Coleman, hoping to get some clue as to why he'd brought me here. I could tell Fanfani of the possibility that Schmidt/ Bach had committed or planned to commit other attacks on women. But what good would it do to confirm his belief, after all this time? Coleman put down his coffee cup and nodded to Fanfani.

157

'Talk to him, Antonio. He's a reasonable man.'

I was glad of the endorsement but still puzzled. Fanfani cleared his throat. 'Rory has told me about the death of the man in Newcastle. The man you believe to have been Werner Schmidt. I understand that you are enquiring into this matter.'

'Yes,' I said.

'I have some information for you. I am willing to give you this information in exchange for something from you.'

'I'm listening.'

'I was very prominent in Rory's organisation. Like him, I demonstrated and talked on the radio. I went to the court, waved banners . . . '

The recollection was taking its toll of him. He faltered, then drew a deep breath and went on. 'My picture was in the newspapers. But, the years have gone by and we have learned to live with our grief, as you see.'

'Yes,' I said, wondering what would come next. The only thing I could think of was that Fanfani and Coleman had someone else to dob in.

'Late last year,' Fanfani said, 'I received a telephone call. It related to Werner Schmidt. There are things about this call that would interest you, Mr Hardy.'

'Such as?'

'Ah, no. Here is where we must strike a deal. If what I tell you leads you to the man who killed Werner Schmidt, you must undertake first, not to harm him and second, to let me talk to him before anyone else—before the lawyers and the police.'

'That could be difficult to arrange, Mr Fanfani.'

'Nevertheless, those are my terms.'

'Would you mind telling me why?'

Fanfani looked stricken. He shook his head and made a gesture to Coleman to take over. Coleman patted Fanfani's shoulder and, although he scarcely moved in his chair, he seemed suddenly to occupy centre stage. 'Antonio does not have very long to live, Mr Hardy. Perhaps a year, perhaps less. The thought of dying without knowing what happened to his daughter, without some certainty in the matter, is deeply troubling to him and to his wife.'

Anger flared in Fanfani, giving him a spurt of energy and spirit. 'The priests tell me to forget my daughter. To compose my soul. I cannot. They are wrong. I must know. I believe that the man who telephoned me knows something about Schmidt and . . . my Angela. I feel it! I must speak with him.'

Coleman's voice was a soothing balm. 'Antonio told me about this telephone call at the time. It was our first contact for many years. I couldn't think of anything to say to him. But when you reached me with your information, it seemed like an intervention . . . You wouldn't understand, Mr Hardy.'

'Probably not,' I said. 'But I can follow up to a point. Mr Fanfani, all I can do is promise you that I'll *try* to arrange things the way you want them. I'll make it a priority.' It was a professional sounding statement but in fact it was totally wild. I meant it, though, more or less. I drained the second can and wished there was another on offer, or something stronger.

'That is fair enough,' Fanfani said. 'I believe that you are a man of honour.'

'I believe that, too,' Coleman said.

So much belief was hard to stomach, especially with nothing but an empty beer can for a prop. I said nothing and sat still.

Fanfani spoke slowly; the hesitation of the non-native speaker getting stronger and making his words almost halting. 'Two things. One, the telephone call. It was made from outside Sydney. I heard the STD beeps. Two . . . do you remember my placards, Rory.'

'Yes,' Coleman said.

Fanfani almost smiled. 'They were written in Italian. I have a better command of strong language in Italian than English. This telephone call, Mr Hardy, was from a man who spoke Italian.'

17

I guess you don't get to be the carpet king without being observant and a shrewd judge of character, and I've never been known for my poker-face. The words were hardly out of Antonio Fanfani's mouth before Coleman jumped in. 'That means something to you, doesn't it, Mr Hardy?'

'It might,' I said. 'Can you tell me exactly what the caller said?'

Fanfani took out a handkerchief and wiped his face. It was cool in the darkened room but he was sweating. 'I cannot remember, exactly. He said something like, "*Abbiamo lo stesso nemico, Antonio.*" '

'I'm sorry,' I said. 'I don't speak Italian.'

Coleman again. ' "We have the same enemy, Antonio." Something like that.'

Fanfani nodded. 'Yes. He was drunk or upset. He said a few more words, but I could hardly hear them and I don't know what they were.'

'Still Italian?'

'I think so.'

'I don't understand,' I said.

'The caller was from the south of Italy or, at least, he spoke in the southern dialect. He might not have been born there. You don't understand these things?'

I shook my head.

'Italian is not like English, Mr Hardy. The one language is not spoken from Palermo to Rimini. The different areas have different languages. They are called dialects but they are more than that. I am from the north.'

He'd fallen into lecturing mode and it was suddenly very irritating. I couldn't help wondering whether this had been part of the problem between him and Angela. 'I find the Glasgow accent pretty hard to understand,' I said, 'also Belfast and Lancashire. What's your point, Mr Fanfani?'

'I have thought very hard about it, but I cannot tell whether this man was old or young. Some of the things he said sounded like childish speech, but some of the Italians born here who do not learn the language properly sound like that. Or it could just be that I am unfamiliar with the southern dialect and do not know what is childish and what is just . . . ' He looked to Coleman for help.

'Slang,' Coleman said.

'Yes. Slang. But this man knows *something!* He knew who I was. Who else could he have meant but Werner Schmidt? I ask you. Who?'

He was getting flushed and excited, showing signs of whatever illness he was suffering from. Of the two men, I had more sympathy for Fanfani. He didn't have Coleman's unctuous

162

style and his pain and guilt were consuming him as much as the disease. I wanted to help him. I got out my pen and pad and made some notes—the private detective's version of the bedside manner. 'I'll be frank with you. What you've told me *does* tie in with my other enquiries.'

'That's good,' Fanfani said.

'Yes. But I'm already working with the police and I may have to . . . '

Fanfani and Coleman exchanged looks. Coleman nodded.

'I understand that you can't do anything criminal, Mr Hardy,' Fanfani said. 'But I beg you to consider my position. I only want to *talk!* I am prepared to engage you . . . '

'I already have a client.'

'Would there be a conflict of interest?' Coleman asked smoothly.

'I don't know.'

Fanfani used the handkerchief again and then put it aside as if denying his weaknesses. 'Let me put it another way. I have many friends in the Newcastle area, especially among the Italian community there. This could be of great help to you, wouldn't you say?'

You didn't have to be a member of Mensa to pick up the implied threat. *Great*, I thought, *the way I'm going I'll have crowbars coming at me from all directions.*

Fanfani saw the way I'd taken it and hastened to put the other side. 'I know men who can protect you, watch places, follow people. Very useful men.'

163

I had to admit that *did* sound useful. The whole business had got very complicated and I needed time and more congenial surroundings to think it through. I stood up. 'Thanks for the drink, Mr Fanfani. I'll think over what you've told me.'

'Think of me, Mr Hardy, and of my wife. We have suffered enough.'

'You realise that none of this may connect up. It could all be coincidence and misunderstanding.'

Fanfani's lean, eroded head nodded. 'But I do not think so. And neither do you. Rory will give you my telephone numbers. Thank you for your time, Mr Hardy.'

Coleman stood, too. He shook hands with Fanfani and ushered me out of the room. We walked down the passages and stairs and I caught glimpses of the bush. The late afternoon sky had darkened as if a storm was moving in. Mrs Fanfani didn't appear and we let outselves out.

'What're your thoughts?' Coleman said as we walked on the circles towards front gate.

'A very unhappy man,' I said. 'He just rang you, did he? Out of the blue?'

'Yes,' Coleman said. 'I see what you're getting at. No, he hasn't had any wild theories over the years. No use of clairvoyants. None of that. He's a very good man. He sounds bitter now, but he's given thousands to the church.'

'Uh huh. What was the trouble between him and the daughter? Anything specific, apart from the contraceptives?'

164

'It was over a boy, of course. He was a student at a school near Angela's. She went to the convent, of course. I don't know how far it had gone but you heard him. We fathers of daughters ... we transfer our own feelings ... I've read a great deal about it. It's very complicated.'

We stood on the side of the road. No sign of Richard or the Merc. 'The cops checked out the boy?'

'Of course. Exhaustively. He was born here but of Italian parents ... '

'Let me guess,' I said. 'From the south?'

'Yes.'

'Give me strength.'

The Mercedes cruised up and Richard jumped out to open the back door for us. Coleman slid into the seat and I slammed the door.

'Mind if I ride up front with you, Richard?'

'Not at all, sir.'

'I get carsick in the back sometimes,' I said.

'Very unpleasant for you, sir.'

'Right. No good for the leather either.'

Thanking Rory Coleman was like trying to eat custard with a fork. It was all 'god's will' and god's work' and in the end 'godspeed'. I drove away from Nuke Castle with a sense of relief and a desperate need for some good, honest sin. The nearest and cheapest sin was a pub in Sutherland I remembered from when I'd had a case in the area. A teenage runaway had been tormenting her parents by making raids on the house, leaving booby-traps and breaking things. The super-respectable parents hadn't wanted the cops involved and I'd had to hang around the neighbourhood for a few weeks until I caught her.

The beer garden of this pub had been a perfect watching post and I'd soaked up a fair bit of expense account beer in the sun. It hadn't been a bad job, especially when it turned out the kid had wanted to be caught anyway. I drove to the pub, which hadn't changed much. I bought a small carafe of white wine and a couple of sandwiches and took them out into the beer garden. It was late in the afternoon and there were only three other drinkers, a man and a woman in deep conversation and an elderly man drinking champagne. They seemed to want to mind their own business and so did I. I sat where I'd sat before but the clear view to the house I'd staked out had gone. Trees and bushes had grown bigger with the passing years. I wondered if the family was still there. Probably not.

I figured I could drink the wine slowly, eat the sandwiches, sit and think a while and not be over the .05 limit. A responsible citizen. It's getting harder to be a sinner. It was cool in the beer garden but the storm I'd anticipated was blowing over the way it can in Sydney. The dark clouds were moving fast towards the eastern horizon and big patches of open, bright sky promised well for tomorrow. I chewed and swallowed, jotted some more notes, underlined things and crossed things out. It's all a substitute for smoking. It doesn't mean a thing.

By the time I'd finished the wine and food and visited the toilet and washed my face and rejected the idea of another drink, I had a few things more or less straight. Odds were, Fanfani's caller was Renato Costi. He fitted the picture in some ways—Australian-born so maybe his Italian wasn't so flash, a boozer, a bad boy. It was enough to go on, a star to steer by. I could ask Glen Withers to check him out. Against every good principle of investigation, I was building a case against him. I went on doing it as I drove back to Glebe. Maybe he had a record for intimidation and extortion Maybe he'd been putting the squeeze on Bach and things had gone wrong—the ground shaking underfoot at just the wrong moment.

I drove badly, shaken myself by thoughts of desperate fathers, lovers and friends. Sometimes it seemed that my work threw me in at the deep end with all the floundering lovers and haters and left me to thrash around, trying to save a few of them, and myself. I realised that I was tired and not thinking anything useful. I occupied myself for the rest of the drive with impressions of Glen Withers—her smell and the texture of her skin, how it had felt as our bodies slapped together. That kept me occupied for the rest of the way to Glebe. I went into the house warmed by the recollections and looking forward to ringing her. The cat wasn't around, there was no mail, nothing to distract me. I took out my notebook, stripped off my jacket and threw it in the direction of the hooks on the wall under the stairs. Sometimes I hit, sometimes I don't. This time I missed. There was a dull thump and I remembered that I'd put my pistol in the pocket of the jacket as I left the car. Sloppy. I went to the phone. There was one message on the answering machine. I pushed play as I opened the notebook to look for Glen's number.

My voice delivered the message, the beep sounded and then Helen's voice came through: 'Cliff. Helen. I'm sorry for the way I left it when we spoke. Give me a call, hey? I'd like to hear from you and the latest on the Jacobs case. Hope you're having fun.'

I was reaching for the phone when a punch landed in the region of my kidneys and a kick collapsed my right knee. I went down and a voice said, 'Fun's over, Cliff.'

18

It's strange the way physical attack affects you. Sometimes you just go under, recognising superior force and hoping to fight another day. Or you kick back against the same odds and take a bad beating. Other times, training, anger, desperation or something else cut in and you can't be stopped. I was tired, stressed, in a confused state of sexual excitement and not ready to lie down for anyone. I came back up off the floor, ricked knee and all, and threw myself against Ralph Jacobs as if I wanted to hammer him through the wall.

I hit him hard and low in his softening gut. There was a whoosh as the air went out of him and I hit him again, higher, wilder, hurting my hand against bone. I yelled and used the pain and the momentum I had to butt him, elbow him, bring my knee up, all in a sequence that would have delighted Sergeant O'Malley. Ralph had no answer. He staggered back, bleeding and defensive and I hacked his feet out from under him with a sweep that brought him down. I fell over myself as the knee gave out.

This might have spoiled the effect except that I landed near where my jacket lay on the floor. I realised then that I hadn't just missed the pegs—I'd hit Ralph as he waited under the stairs. So what? I pulled the Smith & Wesson out of the pocket and jammed it up into the blood flowing from Ralph's nose.

'You're wrong, Ralphie,' I said, 'the fun's just beginning. See these?' I touched the cuts on my face. 'Your boy with the crowbar gave them to me.' I jiggled the gun. 'How about I work you over a bit with this by way of return?'

Ralph's first expression had more of surprise than anything else. I don't suppose the Wrecker had lost many one-on-ones over the years. But now fear was showing in his fleshy, well-tended face. Blood was dripping onto his shirt and the fancy cream cotton jacket and the pressure I was keeping on the gun was hurting his nose cartilage. It was also stopping him from speaking so I eased off a little.

'Do I call the police and charge you with break and enter and assault, or do we talk?'

He ground out one word. 'Talk.'

I gave him a light shove as I took the gun out of his face and edged away from him in a half-crouch. Okay. I haven't shot anyone in my own house in years. It's messy afterwards and I don't like cleaning up. But I'll do it if you give me any trouble. Get over there and sit down.'

I motioned him to a chair in the corner of the room. He dragged himself a metre or so and then seemed to regain enough self-respect to straighten up and complete the trip in an almost normal posture. He was still shaky though, and glad to sit down. I wasn't in much better shape myself. I made it to another chair without actually hobbling, but the back of my leg hurt like hell and I was sore where the kidney punch had landed.

I rubbed the sore spot. 'You better hope I don't piss blood, Ralph. I get very angry when someone causes me to piss blood. Now what the hell's this all about?'

He wiped his face with the back of his hand, saw the blood and dug in the pocket of his jacket for a handkerchief. He found one, but got a lot of gore on the jacket. 'I spoke to Mum on the phone today. She said you got Dad all upset. He's very sick. I warned you to keep off.'

'Did she tell you she'd hired me to go on looking into Oscar Bach's death?'

'No. I . . . '

'Sounds like you did more talking than listening. Your nose is bleeding again.'

He lifted the handkerchief. I flexed my leg and put the gun down on the floor beside the chair. We were both crocks, too old for this game. 'I should've brought someone with me,' he growled.

'How'd you know I'd be coming here?'

'Kept tabs on you all day. You saw the Toyota but I had another car pick you up after that. What've you been doing down south? Anything to do with my old man?'

'Hold on,' I said. 'You've been following me all day? Reporting in by car phone, that sort of thing?' He nodded and some more blood flowed.

'Why?'

'I do a bit of that as a sort of sideline. Favours for people. I put a man on you to give him some practice.'

'Shit, Ralph, you've got some nasty habits. Let me tell you what's going on.'

I told him in some detail, partly to straighten things out for myself, partly because I wanted him off my back, once and for all. He listened, nodding occasionally. I left out the names although they were clear enough in my mind— Gina Costi, Renato 'Ronny' Costi, Mark Roper, Angela Fanfani. I finished and he didn't say anything.

'Family man, are you?' I said.

'Two boys, two girls.'

'How does it grab you, then?'

'I knew that Oscar was creepy. Only met him once, but I knew. I can't understand how Dad got taken in by him.'

'You've got too simple a view of human nature, Ralph. I've known some real nice blokes who liked doing very nasty things when the mood was on them.'

'And Mum wants you to find out who did him? You'll tell Dad and everything'll be okay?'

'What d'you reckon?'

He shook his head. 'I don't know. It's beyond me. I never thought our family'd get involved in anything like this.'

I suppose it was then that I warmed a bit towards Ralph Jacobs. He came clean with me,

172

admitted that he was a bit strapped for cash and had been hoping to put the bite on his father. He didn't want anyone siphoning off the loot, like a private detective who might bleed the old man for months or even blackmail him. He said the crowbar kid had exceeded his orders which, given the kidney punch and the knee kick, I doubted. But Ralph wasn't a happy man. I could sense that he was under pressure—business or personal, or both.

'Your mother's holding things together up there,' I said. 'I think she could use a bit of help.'

He nodded. 'Never seem to find the time. I'll try. You reckon you know who it was, this wog?'

'Show a bit of class, Wrecker,' I said. 'Didn't you ever meet an Italian who could run the bloody legs off you?'

He grinned. 'Yeah, yeah, sure I did. And tackle, too. Okay, this Italian.'

'I've got an idea. But I'm going to have to go carefully.'

'Maybe I could help.'

I sighed. 'Ralph, I've got the man down south ready and willing to help. He's a builder. I fancy he could swing a few cement mixers my way. You've got friends with Toyotas and car phones and iron bars . . . '

'I said he was out of line. I'll talk to him.'

'Don't bother. If I ever see him again without the crowbar we'll have a chat. My point is, I'm working with the police on this and . . . '

Ralph's grin was a bit lopsided and all the

173

more salacious for that. 'Yeah, Senior Sergeant Withers. She's a goer, I'm told.'

That's when I told him to piss off. He'd recovered a lot of his aplomb by this time. He stood up, took a card from his pocket and set it down on the chair. 'You can reach me,' he said. 'And, Hardy, the locks on this place are lousy. Yours took me about thirty seconds and I'm no expert.'

I said, 'You see anything worth stealing?' But he was gone.

When I got out of the chair the pain really hit me. My back felt as if it was on fire and the knee was going to need strapping. I staggered to the toilet but there was no blood. Lucky for Ralph. The bath is old and stained but it's deep and I can submerge myself in it up to the shoulders. That's what I did, in water as hot as I could stand it and with a couple of inches of scotch to hand. I breathed in the steam and tried to think *open pores, get ye hence toxins, circulate blood, heal wounds*. When the water cooled I let some out and ran in some more hot. I was probably in there an hour and felt better at the end of it, although whether it was the bath, the healing thoughts or the scotch that did the trick was hard to say.

I decided that it was the scotch and had some more. A few painkillers didn't seem like a bad idea either and after that my bed felt like a cloud. I drifted off into a doped sleep. The cat scratched at the balcony window and I laughed at it. The phone rang and I ignored it. I dreamed I was young again and running to catch a Bondi tram. I'd almost got my hand on the rail when the strength left my legs and the tram pulled away and I stood in the middle of the tracks watching it go.

19

There wasn't much of the morning left when I
woke up and what there was of it was pretty
nasty. The storm of last night must have moved
out to sea and come back again, bigger and
better. The sky was dark and the wind and rain
were lashing at the trees that overgrow my balcony. I struggled out of bed, pulled on a
tracksuit and went downstairs to make coffee
and see if the cat had survived the night. It had,
of course. The house is even more vulnerable
than Ralph Jacobs thought. The cat had found a
way in through a broken section of fibro in the
bathroom wall. It was curled up asleep close to
the hot water service. Smart cat.

With the coffee came normalcy. Which is to
say, confusion. I had enquiries to make in
Newcastle and a source of official help—Glen
Withers, who by now might have found out
other things herself. Then there was Horrie and
May and Ralph and Antonio, all expecting
things of me and likely to be disappointed. I
could have done with some sunshine but the
sky stayed dark even though the rain and wind

176

eased a little. I saw myself driving north on the fairly new steel-belted radials. And then what? I reached for the phone to call Glen and saw that the message light wasn't blinking. I must have hit the reset button by accident when Ralph hit me, deliberately. Through the fog of the encounter with Ralph and the drugged sleep, I tried to remember Helen's message. 'Call me, hey?' was as much as I could recall. Welcoming. More confusion.

I dialled Glen's work number and waited an age before the phone was picked up. Male voice. 'Sergeant Withers' phone.'

'I'm calling from Sydney. Is Sergeant Withers around?'

'What is it in connection with, sir?'

'I'm not at liberty to say.'

'Sergeant Withers is in a meeting. Can I get her to call you back?'

'No,' I said. 'Tell her I'm on my way to Newcastle and that I'll call her when I arrive.'

His tone changed from the one he used for the innocent public to the one for the villains and fizzgigs. 'What name?'

'Write this down,' I said. 'Oscar Jacob Dudley Schmidt.'

'Would you care to spell that?'

I hung up and went off to shave and to locate some clean clothes. A little of Ralph's blood had got on the shirt and trousers I'd been wearing yesterday. I felt some satisfaction when I saw it. I was getting a little tired of being pushed around, threatened and offered blandishments. I felt like doing some pushing back

177

and a Newcastle lair bikie seemed as good a subject as any. I knew it was all displaced sexual energy working, but what the hell? You have to do something with it.

It was hard to believe I'd been getting sunburned on Redhead Beach a few days before. The rain lashed down all the way up the North Shore and for most of the way to Gosford. I drove carefully but impatiently. I tried the radio but the ABC annoyed me—I felt I'd heard all the talk and opinions and recipes for improvement a hundred times before—and the commercial stations made me want to be on a desert island where no radio wave could ever reach. Plus my back ached. I broke a rule of some years' standing and had a swig of rum at 10.30 a.m. My old Mum always said I'd join her in the other place—in Nick's pub, most likely.

The weather cleared after Gosford and by Wyong the sun was making the road steam and I was hot inside my shirt and denim jacket. Impossible to please. I shrugged out of the jacket as I drove and lost a little control, to the justified annoyance of a truckie, who tooted me and gave me the finger as he streamed past.

I diverged off the freeway at the Newcastle sign and hadn't gone more than a half kilometre before the motor cycle cop picked me up. I checked the speedo and swore. I'd been a fraction over the speed limit, encouraged by the dry road with no traffic on it. I slowed as he hit the siren and roared up beside me, making a macho 'pull over' sign with his black-gloved hand. I sometimes have a problem with authority when it's wearing black leather boots, but sanity prevailed. I slowed down and pulled over like a good, solid citizen.

The cop's boots crunched on the gravel. 'May I see your licence, sir?'

I handed him the plastic card with the photograph that makes me look like a Long Bay resident on day release. He examined it carefully. 'Do you have a weapon, Mr Hardy?'

That was unusual and I took a closer look at him to make sure he was the genuine article. Cap, vizor up as per regulations, badge in evidence, youngish face carrying a little too much fat. The real thing. I opened the glove box and let him see the .38 sitting there inside its holster. 'I'm licensed to carry it,' I said.

'Not concealed.'

'It's in the glove box, for Christ's sake. What is this?'

'Please hand me the weapon.'

'Why?'

'I have instructions to escort you to Police Headquarters in Newcastle,' he said. 'No private citizen entering the building is permitted to carry a weapon.'

'Why, again?'

'I'm simply obeying orders, Mr Hardy. If you surrender the weapon you can drive in and everything will be all right. If you resist, I'll call for help and you'll be placed under restraint and someone else will drive your car. Either way, you and the gun won't be together. Which is it to be, sir?'

The 'sir' was heavily ironical. He wasn't as much of an android as he liked to pretend. I gave him marks for that and passed the pistol out through the open window. Quick as a flash I pulled out a felt pen and scribbled on my wrist. 'I've got your badge number, son,' I said. 'I hope your saddlebag hasn't got a hole in it.'

He snapped the vizor down. 'Follow me, Mr Hardy.'

Quick trip. I was parking the car inside the 'reserved for police' section within the hour. The motor cycle cop escorted me to the front desk and handed my pistol over to a civilian clerk who made an entry in a ruled book. One black leather finger touched his cap and he was gone. I was ushered into a lift and up several floors to a conference room. Sitting around the big table with carafes of water and the leavings of a morning tea were two men and a woman

Detective Inspector Withers looked a bit the worse for wear and tear; his tie knot had slipped down and his collar was wrinkled. He hung up a telephone, one of three on the table, as I came in. His daughter looked pretty fresh. The other man at the table was a thin, beak-nosed individual in an elaborate cop uniform with lots of brass and braid. No-one stood up when I entered which didn't surprise me. I nodded at the two members of the Withers family and sat down at the table a few places away from any of them.

'This is Assistant Commissioner Morton, Mr Hardy,' Edward Withers said.

I nodded in the direction of the brass and braid. 'Aren't you going to introduce me to him?'

'I know who you are, Mr Hardy,' Morton said. 'I've heard all about you from your friends and enemies in Sydney.'

'Always good to get a balanced view,' I said. 'Would someone tell me what this is all about? I was doing ninety-seven in a ninety-five zone, but I hardly think that could be it.'

Withers sighed. 'I told you he was a smartarse, Leslie.'

I looked at Morton who was reading notes on a pad in front of him. He seemed not to hear what Withers had said. The arrogance of command.

'I'll call you Les,' I said. 'I don't take too kindly to being disarmed and escorted into town by an SS type who likes to admire his face in his shiny boots, Les. You tell me what this is about right now, or I walk out and phone my lawyer and a reporter or two.'

Glen shot me a surprised and angry look and I favoured her with one of my best smiles—one with a bit of the back pain and broken nose in it but with lots of promise of laughs to come. She sat back and didn't react.

'Take it easy, Hardy,' Morton said smoothly. 'The boy may have been a bit over-eager, but better that than sloppy. Wouldn't you agree?'

181

I got to my feet. 'I said I wanted explanations, not blarney.'

'Oscar Bach may have killed four women,' Glen blurted out. 'Maybe more.'

I sat down and shut up and let them tell it. Glen had checked on the four locations marked on the map and come up with missing females, foul play suspected, in each. The circumstances tallied pretty closely with the details of the crime for which Werner Schmidt had been convicted. The females, teenagers, girls, had been last seen on roads around the districts in which they lived. There had been the usual sightings of strangers and vehicles, but the disappearances had remained unsolved. Common to three of the cases was the sighting of a dusty Bedford panel van. Withers slid a piece of paper across towards me—on it was written three different versions of the van's number plate. I got out my notebook. One of the numbers was way off, but the others were within a digit or two of the number of Oscar Bach's van.

'We've got a big problem, Hardy,' Morton said. 'Nobody'll be happy about sheeting these crimes home to a dead man. The relations of the victims least of all.'

Withers tapped his shirt pocket as if feeling for cigarettes. Then he shook his head. He exchanged glances with his daughter, who wasn't smoking either. I guessed that Ted had quit and Glen approved.

'They'll feel cheated of their revenge,' Withers said.

Glen tidied the papers in front of her. 'It's

more than that. The friends and relations want some details.'

'Ghouls,' Withers said.

'No, Dad . . . Inspector. It's not ghoulish. They need to know in order to get over it. To rule a line.'

I nodded at that and Morton evidently thought the time was right for me to contribute. 'Right, Hardy. Now what can you tell us?'

'About what?'

'About what you've been doing in Sydney.'

Problem time. I'd given Antonio Fanfani some sort of an undertaking which would be hard to fulfil if I had to spill my guts to the police now. But four more deaths changed things somewhat. I could feel Glen's eyes on me. I tried to remember how much I'd told her about the Costis and couldn't quite do it. Had I given her chapter and verse, all the names?

'Cliff,' she said. 'I had to take it higher up when the locations and probable deaths started to tally up. You understand?'

I nodded. Withers gave us both a long look but Morton chose not to react. 'We need information, Hardy,' he said. 'All we can get. Sergei Costi's an important man in this town and prominent in the Italian community.'

'What about his son, Renato?'

Morton leaned forward. 'Tell us.'

I told them, without giving away any more than I needed to. I told them about Mark Roper's fear of Renato and about the phone call to Fanfani from someone whose Italian wasn't so hot and who might have been drunk.

'Ronny,' Withers said. 'Has to be.'

Glen shuffled papers and found what she wanted. 'But he hasn't come after Roper.'

Morton looked at me.

'Roper's not a very reliable character,' I said. 'Costi might have threatened him or blackmailed him. He mightn't have told me about it. Might have hoped I'd get Ronny off his back in some way.'

'Or,' Morton said, 'after he killed Schmidt he might've got scared and gone quiet. Perhaps he thought he'd squared the account, and going after Roper was unnecessary.'

Withers' body language screamed impatience. He fidgeted, touched his tie knot, re-rolled a shirt sleeve. He wanted to go out and start clapping on handcuffs. Glen's professional attitude was intact but she seemed to be reaching for some other level of understanding. 'Could it be,' she said slowly, 'that Renato's main concern was with his sister's honour, as publicly perceived, and with Bach dead and Roper scared, the dishonour wouldn't become known?'

I could see sense in that, and also danger. But what we were doing now threatened to blow things apart. An irrelevant thought came to me. 'Where's the box and the other stuff?'

'Being analysed,' Morton said. 'Which brings us to the next point. We've put a stop on the work at the Ocean Street house and our blokes have had a quick look. They say there's blood in the bathroom.'

20

The telephone closest to Morton rang and he answered it. He grunted several times. I looked at Glen who gave me a half-smile before play ing with her notes again. *Some ground to make up there*, I thought. Morton put the phone down and shifted in his seat the way chairmen do when the meeting is almost over.

'The Ocean Street house is owned by Sergei Costi,' he said. 'He ordered the renovations to be done.'

'When he heard Cliff was poking around,' Glen said.

Morton nodded. He seemed cool, calm and collected inside his flash uniform, even though it was starting to get warm in the the room. 'As I say, this is very tricky in several directions. I'm declaring this group an informal task force. We have to keep a lid on things for as long as we can.'

'I'm a civilian,' I said. 'You can't declare me an anything, Les.'

'I'm 'asking for your co-operation, Hardy. You've been the thin end of the wedge into this mess. If everything works out all right, the community will be in your debt.'

'You're a politician.'

'I'm an Assistant Commissioner of Police,' Morton said. 'If I weren't a politician, I'd be a Senior Constable in Woop Woop. I also want to appeal to your better instincts. This community has been through a lot—the earthquake, the bus crash up north—it's under strain and doesn't need any more bad news. Don't get me wrong, I don't want to cover anything up, I just don't want rumours, and reporters going off half-cocked and citizens getting scared.'

'I'll play,' I said. 'But I have to tell you that I've got a commitment to a client to let him talk to the man who killed Oscar Bach. He's hoping for the sort of information the Senior Sergeant here was talking about before.'

'Noted,' Morton said. 'We'll see what we can do. For now, I want you, Senior Sergeant, to locate the Costi girl and have a talk with her. We need to know whether she told her brother about what had happened and how he reacted.'

'Yes, sir,' Glen said.

'I'm going to tackle Sergei. Not directly, of course. I'll come at him through a few of our mutual acquaintances. For the moment, we leave Renato Costi alone, beyond making sure we know where he is.'

'Do we know that now?' I said.

Morton looked at Withers who shook his head. 'It's being seen to,' he said.

'Right.' Morton half-rose from his chair and then sat back. 'You don't look happy, Mr Hardy.'

'I'm not,' I said. 'What do you expect me to do while you're all running around being official?'

'I want you to stay close to Detective Inspector Withers. He's going out to supervise the work at Ocean Street. I think you might find that interesting.'

I annoyed Withers by insisting on reclaiming my pistol at the desk and strapping it on. To my surprise, Morton accompanied us to the car park and shook hands with me before going about his business. The drive to Dudley wasn't the most comfortable I'd ever taken. I tried to think whether I'd had any dealings with the fathers of women I'd been involved with since I was about eighteen, and couldn't come up with any. We exchanged a few grunts about the weather and Morton's style of doing things. As if by mutual agreement, neither of us mentioned Glen, but she was in the minds of both of us. Withers had freshened himself up a bit and I fancied there was a slight tang of whisky about him. Very slight. We sat in the back of the car and let a constable do the driving.

I was under no illusions as to why I was accompanying Withers—Morton had teamed us up to prevent me going off and doing anything on my own. Withers stared out the window. He sighed and turned his head towards me. 'I'm three years from my pension,' he said too quietly for the driver, a youth who looked fresh from the Academy, to hear.

187

'Good for you.'

'I don't want anything to fuck up.'

'Understandable.'

'Do you know what I'm saying?'

'Not exactly, no.'

Another sigh. 'Sergei Costi's been around for a long time. He's had his fingers in a lot of pies.'

'Business is like that,' I said. 'I'm a small businessman myself.'

'Don't play dumb with me, Hardy,' Withers hissed. 'You know what I'm driving at.'

'I'm a bit slow, Ted. Spell it out for me.'

'It wouldn't be easy to squeeze Costi hard— he'd be able to squeeze back.'

'What about Ronny?'

'With that mob—same thing. Hurt one, you hurt 'em all. I'm worried.'

'For your pension?'

'Yeah, but not only that.' He touched his shirt pocket again with the same result as before. 'Shit, I stopped smoking a couple of weeks back. Glen's idea. I dunno . . . I can't seem to think straight since.'

The name had been spoken and it seemed to break some kind of knot in Withers. He tapped the constable on the shoulder, botted a cigarette from him and lit up. 'Jesus, that's better. Turn on the radio, son, and keep yourself amused. Me and Mr Hardy are talking old farts' stuff back here.'

The radio came on and Withers spoke quickly and urgently. He was worried, he said, about Glen. If things got sticky between the police and Sergei Costi it was more than likely

188

that Costi would go down. He would under-stand that as well as anyone. 'I don't want Glen around if it gets to that point. If she's with the Costi girl and everything blows up, who knows how it might all sort out? I'm going out on a limb here, Hardy, talking to you like this.'

'I know,' I said.

'You care about Glen?'

I nodded. 'But I still don't know where you're pointing.'

Withers shrugged, took a last deep drag on the cigarette and threw the butt out the window. 'Neither do I. But I wanted to put you in the picture. With a bit of luck, everything'll sort out okay. If it gets rough, I'm looking after Glen first and myself second. Got it?'

I didn't reply. We zoomed through Kahiba and the constable threw the car into the last roundabout and roared up through Whitebridge towards Dudley.

'Turn the fuckin' radio off and slow down,' Withers snarled.

There was a fair-sized crowd assembled outside 88 Ocean Street—gawkers, police forensic men, Jeff, the renovator and his mate who'd been stopped in their tracks. Withers pushed through and I followed him down the side path to the back of the house. The activity and the number of people around made the place seem smaller and meaner. The backyard was stacked with galvanised iron, floorboards, masonite and other materials. The big bath, looking like a

189

beached whale, sat on its claw legs in the middle of a patch of sunlight. I was surprised that they hadn't found a reason to chop down the trees.

Withers nodded to a few of the men and got a cigarette from one of them. 'What the fuck's this?' he said, pointing at a portable power unit that had been wheeled into place. Cigarettes seemed to increase his energy but not improve his humour.

A man, whose white overall couldn't conceal that he was a cop, held a light to Withers' cigarette. 'The old lady next door's been useful, Inspector. She reckons there's a well under this concrete.' With his boot he scuffed the slab that covered the space between the house and the bathroom. 'Her place has one and she says all these houses did in the old days. A section of the slab looks fairly new.'

'So it does,' Withers said. 'All right. Get on with it.'

It was hot in the backyard, even under the trees, and the hammering and battering made it feel even hotter. Someone went off for sandwiches and soft drinks but I was a civilian, even if I had been co-opted, and I brought back a couple of cans of light beer. They were trying to work around the new section of slab in order to lever it out but it was thick and had some reinforcing rods through it. The work was interrupted by frequent conferences between the jackhammer operators and Jeff. The backyard filled with gritty dust that settled on the grass, making it grey and mottled. Not a cheerful place to begin with, 88 Ocean Street was getting more depressing by the minute.

Molly from next door hung over the fence taking in every detail of the scene. She recognised me and beckoned me across.

'I knew he was a wrong 'un,' she said.

'How come?'

'Never even had a washing machine,' she said. 'Washed his clothes in the bath and hung them on the line there.' She pointed to a slack length of clothes line strung between two trees at the back of the block. 'Always washing his clothes, he was. And never bought a washing machine.'

'Was he friendly, Molly? Did you chat much?'

'Nah. Never gave me the time of day. Wouldn't have talked to him for more than a minute or two a couple of times in the whole three or four years he was there.'

'What did he talk about, when he did talk?'

'Are you with the police? I seen you here with Horrie Jacobs the other day.'

'I'm helping the police. Can you remember what Mr Bach talked about?'

She scratched her thin grey hair and re-adjusted her spectacles on her nose. Her eyes were still very blue for an elderly person and despite the specs I had the feeling they wouldn't have missed much. Her hearing was sound too, because she could follow what I was saying over all the racket just a few metres away. 'Didn't say much. I remember he was very interested in the lagoon. I told him where it was and how to get there.'

191

'The lagoon?'

She jerked her thumb over her shoulder, indicating the direction of the football ground and beyond. 'Redhead lagoon, that way a mile or so. Lovely spot. You walk through the Awabakal reserve and . . .'

A shout from the work site interrupted her. She craned forward over the fence. The slab had cracked diagonally and they had lifted one of the sections free to expose the top of the well.

It was almost comical to see the way every man gathered around the hole jumped back. I walked across and found out why before I'd taken more than four steps—the stink coming up from below was foul and cloying. It seemed to be almost a physical thing, like a gas and be reaching out to wrap itself around you and go up your nostrils and into your mouth to fill your head with corruption.

Withers was the first to do anything. 'Torch,' he snapped. Someone handed him a big battery pack flashlight and he advanced to the hole and shone it down. I found a handkerchief in my pocket and tied it across my face before I joined Withers at the well. In the strong beam of light I saw that the well had bricked sides and was about twenty feet deep, maybe more. The walls were slimy and grey-green. I stared down, trying not to breathe, and could just make out something lumpy and misshapen at the bottom. It looked like a couple of bags of rubbish. Withers moved the torch and the light reflected off heavy, dark plastic. The bags sat in several centimetres of grey ooze. The smell seemed to get worse.

Withers stepped back and looked over to where one of the cops was pulling on heavy rubber boots and gloves and a plastic overall. Withers tossed him the torch. 'Have fun,' he said.

The team got busy rigging up some tackle to permit things to go down into the well and come up again. Withers and I retired to the shade of a tree near the rough brick barbeque. Withers had evidently sent out for cigarettes because he now had a pack and a lighter of his own. He lit up and blew smoke up into the branches of the tree. I untied the handkerchief and wiped my face with it. After the stink from the pit, the tobacco smoke smelled almost good.

'Leslie Morton's going to love this,' Withers said. 'This is just what we need. We've had a serial killer living in our midst for a couple of years and it takes a dago kid worried about his sister's cherry to take care of him.'

'Inspector,' one of the cops yelled. 'Press.'

Withers lit another cigarette from the stub of his last. 'Tell 'em to piss off. No-one gets in here. No pictures. Understand?'

There was a little commotion at the side of the house and some voices were raised. Something was being lifted clear of the well.

'Fuck it,' Withers said. 'This is going to blow sky high.'

'Can you get in touch with Glen? She shouldn't get too close to the Costis, not if the

193

press starts to sort out what's going on here.'

'You're right.' Withers summoned our driver over and issued instructions to him to contact Senior Sergeant Withers and get her to report in. The cop, looking relieved to be getting away from what was going on in the backyard, hurried off to do his bidding. Withers lit another cigarette and we went across to where activity around the hole had stopped. Two heavy plastic garbage bags, covered in slime, lay on the cement. Both had been torn; a human knee, or part of a knee, stuck out of the hole in one bag; from the other a hand protruded. The smell was like ammonia and rotting fish combined.

'Jesus Christ,' Withers said. 'But only two?'

That's when I told him about Oscar Bach's interest in the Redhead lagoon.

21

The media were not to be denied. TV crews, radio units and print persons arrived, drawn to the scene like kids to a schoolyard fight. Their behaviour wasn't so different either. They jostled and shouted, abused the police who struggled to keep them back, and started filming and photographing everything in sight. The neighbours, mostly elderly women, had never received so much attention in their lives. They revelled in it, inviting the reporters in for cups of tea and talking non-stop.

Withers floundered. He tried shouts and threats of arrest, but arrest at a news point is a badge of honour for reporters these days, and they ignored him. He did manage to keep the cameras out of the backyard of number 88, but they were operating from Molly's place—her yard and roof—so it didn't make much difference. The youngster who'd been detailed to contact Glen came pushing through the throng, struggling to get Withers' attention. He got mine first.

'What's up?' I said.

He was red-faced, sweating and worried. He had to tell someone, but was I the right person to tell? He decided I was. 'I can't raise Sergeant Withers. Her radio's emitting an alarm signal.'

'What does that mean?'

Again, he looked doubtful about revealing professional things to a civilian. But Withers was in a shouting match with a TV cameraman and he had no choice. 'An officer can activate an alarm signal that'll be picked up when another unit tries to contact him. That's what we're getting.'

'Can you home in on the signal?'

'Yes, but I should talk to Inspector Withers. . .'

'Look at him,' I said. 'He's got his hands full. And I have to tell you this, Constable . . . ?'

'Drewe.'

'Constable Drewe. You saw me shake hands with Assistant Commissioner Morton, didn't you?'

'Yes, but . . . '

'He co-opted me to keep an eye on the Inspector because Senior Sergeant Withers is involved in this case and he was worried about her father's objectivity. D'you follow me?'

'I'm not sure.'

I pushed him back down the path. 'Come on, Constable. Show some initiative. You can call in whatever other help you like, but the Inspector's better out of this.'

'I dunno . . . '

I showed him the holster. 'Look, they gave me my gun back and all. We can reach Morton

196

and he'll confirm what I'm saying. But we have to be quick!'

Drewe's dislike of Withers probably gave me the edge. He suddenly became all business, pushed past the people congregating outside in the street and beckoned me over to the squad car. He twiddled with knobs, tried calling Glen, and got a hum. 'Get in,' he said. 'She isn't far off.'

'I know where she is,' I slammed the door and ignored a few interested looks from reporters. 'Sergei Costi's house in Kahiba. Know it?'

'Who doesn't?'

He gunned the motor and took off quickly, forcing the interested reporters to jump out of the way. Constable Drewe was born to drive— he handled the car as if it was an extension of his body and he was connected to it with nerves and blood vessels. He drove very fast and I felt very safe. We went down Burwood Road, past the elaborate houses and Glen's cottage and onto the stretch of road where the forest surrounds the few residences set on five-acre blocks. The hum got louder and Drewe pointed. A Honda Civic with police markings stood under a tree by the side of the dirt track that led off the main road towards the entrance to the Costi house.

Taking my second look at it, Sergei Costi's house made those of Rory Coleman and Antonio Fanfani look cheap. There was something solid about it, as if it was rooted to the earth and all the new, fast money that might float around wouldn't buy a brick of it. Except, of course, that it was fairly new and no doubt fairly fast money that *had* bought it.

Big pine trees grew close to the house on the south side and the ocean was visible away to the west. The sky had cleared completely and the house was bathed in sunshine. From this angle, I could see a swimming pool and a tennis court. There were two cars drawn up on the wide, bricked driveway. The only incongruous thing was the big, black motor bike parked contemptuously in the middle of the drive, blocking both cars.

Drewe went across to the Honda and peered inside. 'It's her car. What d'we do now?'

The big house looked unnaturally quiet and still. *Why wasn't anyone playing tennis or swimming? Where was the chauffeur and the under-gardener?* 'Try and get in touch with Morton,' I said. 'I don't like the feel of this.'

Drewe got busy on the radio. I could hear the squawks and buzzes and the sound of agitated exchanges. I stood beside the car, leaning on the opened passenger door, and watched the house. Nothing moved. Then I heard Drewe. 'Mr Hardy, I've got through to the Assistant Commissioner. He's telling us to get . . . '

A sharp crack, like the sound of stockwhip, and the windscreen of the police car exploded. Drewe yelled as he was showered with glass. The bullet had missed my head by a few centimetres and I nearly dislocated every joint in my body getting down and under cover behind the door. 'Drewe! You okay?'

'Yeah. Cut a bit. Blood everywhere, but I think it's just nicks. Shit!'

He was crouched low, half in and half out of the car. The radio buzzed angrily and he gave his call sign and reported that he'd been fired on. 'Hunter, Victor, Bravo. Superficial wounds,' he said. 'Awaiting instructions, over.'

'What's happening?' I said.

He waved me silent and listened. 'Roger, out.' He put the handset back on its cradle. A red light blinked angrily. 'Reinforcements coming. Commissioner Morton'll be here.'

'But what's going on?'

'Officer down,' he said. 'Sergeant Withers. That's all I know. I'm only a fucking constable, Mr Hardy. Do you really think they'd tell *me*?'

'What about Inspector Withers?'

'If he shows up I'm instructed to tell him to leave the area, on Commissioner Morton's auth ority. Fat fucking chance. I just hope Morton gets here first. We're supposed to withdraw now. Come on.'

'I'm staying here. I've got an idea where that shot came from. You should go and get those cuts looked at.'

'Fuck you,' he said. He edged clear of the door and worked his way towards the back of the car. There was another whipping, slapping sound and the car shook.

'Drewe?'

'I'm all right. If he hits the petrol tank . . . '

'Hundred to one against. I've spotted him, I'm pretty sure. How d'you work this radio?'

'Button on the left of the handpiece—depress it to talk, and lift it to receive. The unit's . . .'

'Hunter, Victor, Bravo, I know.'

There was a note of panic in his voice now. 'I've got blood in my eyes. I can't see!'

'Hold on, son,' I said, 'they'll be here in a minute. You've done fine and I'll say so.'

He laughed. *Hysteria coming*, I thought. Then I heard the sound of car tyres on the dirt. Six police cars rolled to a stop on the track. They were shielded from the house by trees but anyone really looking could spot them. I hoped Drewe didn't try to make a break for them—he could get himself shot and draw attention to the cars at the same time. The radio buzzed and I reached over and grabbed it.

'Hunter, Victor, Bravo, this is Hunter Victor King. Are you receiving?'

I pressed the button and said, 'This is Hardy, Mr Morton and I'm not going to go through all that rigmarole. I can hear you. Constable Drewe and I have been under fire from the house. Drewe has some superficial cuts. Now, what can you tell me?'

'A lot,' Morton said. 'Too bloody much. Have you tried to get away from your present position?'

'Drewe tried and nearly got a bullet for his pains. The shooter's at an upstairs window. He's got a pretty good rifle and he can shoot. Does Renato shoot?'

'Yes. I'm told he's also a CB freak, so there's a

200

pretty good chance he'll listen in once he knows we're here. Jesus Christ!'

'What?'

'It's Ted Withers. Somebody stop that car!'

I screwed myself around and saw a car moving fast along the track, past the tree cover and down to where Drewe's car and the Honda were parked. Ted Withers jumped from the car the second it stopped.

'Get down!' I yelled.

He ignored me and began to walk towards the house. The whipping, slapping sound came again and Withers staggered back as if he'd walked into a glass wall I didn't think, I moved. Out of the car, ducking low, almost crawling. I scurried across to where Withers was twitching on the ground. I grabbed his arm and pulled him back into his car. His feet clawed at the ground. I couldn't tell whether he was co-operating or resisting but I pulled him anyway. Another shot sounded but it clanged into the car I'd just left. I hoped Drewe wasn't doing anything foolish. I pushed Withers into the passenger seat of his car and tucked myself in behind the wheel with my head below the dashboard. I turned the ignition, shoved the lever into reverse and put my knee on the accelerator. The door swung wildly and the car slewed and bucked as it roared backwards. I didn't try to steer it beyond keeping the wheel from spinning. Blood was leaking from Withers and getting all over both of us. He was swearing at me and the world.

A bullet whanged off the roof and I heard

someone shout 'Left! Left!' I tugged at the steering wheel and then there was a grinding crunch and we stopped. I fell out of the open door. My first impulse was to try and crawl under the car but a hand gripped my shoulder and guided me back behind the tree I'd slammed into. Morton was there along with several other cops. Then I heard a struggle and more swearing from Withers as he was manhandled back under cover. His face was white and his clothes were soaked with blood but he was still fighting. He saw Morton and stopped struggling.

'Leslie,' he said, 'Glen's in there.'

'I know, Ted. We'll do everything we can. Take it easy till the doctor gets here. I'd say Hardy here saved your life.'

Withers' colour was worse, greyish. He was close to collapse. 'Fuck him,' he said. 'He got her into this fucking mess.' He sagged at the knees and one of the cops gently lowered him to the ground.

'Hardy,' Morton said, 'you all right?'

I was wiping blood from my face with my sleeve. 'Yeah. Where's Drewe?'

'He went sideways when you got Ted's car moving. You bloody nearly ran over him.'

'He did all right,' I said. 'Will you please tell me what's going on?'

Morton wasn't listening to me. He looked across to where a uniformed cop with a rifle fitted with a telescopic sight was squatting, training the weapon on the house. 'I can see him, sir,' the marksman said. 'He's at the open window, top left. But I'll need another couple of square inches of him to be absolutely sure of a shot.'

'Wait,' Morton said.

22

The sequence of events, as Morton gave them to
me, was this: Glen had gone to the house to
interview Gina Costi in order to discover
whether she'd told Renato about Oscar Bach
having raped her. At about the same time
Morton got through to Sergei Costi on the telephone. He outlined the problem in general
terms and asked Costi to come into town for a
discussion. The next bit Morton had to recon-
struct from a panicked and interrupted telephone call from Costi. Renato had overheard
Glen talking to his sister. He had gone crazy
and burst in threatening to kill the girl and
Mark Roper. There had been a struggle and
Glen had been shot. Costi Senior had quickly
rung Morton with the gist of this before his son
had cut him off.

'No communication since then,' Morton said.
'We don't know the condition of Sergeant Withers or the other people in the house. We don't
even know how many people are in there.'

A policeman came scuttling across towards
us, bent low. He glanced hesitantly at me but

Morton made an impatient gesture and he spoke up. 'Sir, we've had a communication from the house. From Renaldo Costi.'

'Renato,' Morton said. 'Go on.'

'He says he wants Mark Roper brought to the house. If he doesn't get here within an hour he's going to kill Sergeant Withers, his mother and father,' he glanced at his notebook, 'Mrs Adamo and himself.'

'Jesus,' Morton said. 'Is the line open to the house?'

'He said he'd cut it off in ten minutes. That's about four minutes ago.'

'Ring it and patch me through from my car. Quick!'

'Sir.' The cop ran off, forgetting to bend over.

Morton looked at me. 'Siege and hostage situation. Terrific.'

'What'll you say to him?'

'Stall him. What else can I do? I can't deliver a citizen up to him like a sacrifice.'

'Substitute?' I said. 'Decoy?'

We moved to one of the police cars and Morton snapped his fingers while an officer fiddled with the radio. 'I was trying not to think about it. What's this Roper look like?'

'Tall, dark, thin, young.'

Morton stood about four inches shorter than me; both of us looked every day of our ages. 'Lets me out, and you.'

'This time of day he'd be wearing a blue overall. He's a pest exterminator.'

Morton nodded. He spoke rapidly to a hovering sergeant who nodded and hurried away.

Then he picked up the radio. 'Mr Costi. This is Assistant Commissioner Leslie Morton. Can you hear me?'

The voice came through loud and clear—young, slightly sing-song, although very Australian. 'This is Ronny Costi. Who'd you say you were?'

'I'm the senior policeman here. We should talk . . . '

'Nothing to talk about, mate. Everything's fucked.'

'It doesn't have to be like that, Mr Costi. Now . . .'

The voice went up into a scream. 'My sister's been raped and that little cunt Roper's told everyone about it and this family's buggered. It's history. I'm going . . . '

Morton must have figured he had nothing to lose. His voice cut across the raving. 'Listen to me! We're getting Mr Roper here. We can talk some more. We'll get your brother too . . . '

'No! Leave him the fuck out of it!'

'Mr Costi! Let me talk to your father.'

Renato let out a stream of curses in Italian and English; I caught only the obvious Italian ones about the Madonna and violating her; the English ones were in the same vein without the religious associations. Morton's knuckles went white as he gripped the radio handpiece. He glanced across at the marksman who was still in position. The marksman shook his head and signalled that he didn't have a target.

Morton tried again. 'Renato, Ronny, listen . . .'

The voice went suddenly calm. 'Shut up,

cunt. Roper better be here fuckin' soon, or we'll all be dead and I just might get a few of you cunts out there as well.'

The connection broke. Morton handed the radio to the policeman who'd operated it before. He called the central communications room, spoke briefly, waited and shook his head. 'Line's dead, sir. He's cut it.'

A shot from the house. The windscreen of the Honda Glen had driven disintegrated. Another shot screamed off the roof of the car and whistled away into the trees.

'He's back at the window,' the marksman said. 'But I still can't get a big enough piece of him. I could try . . . '

'No,' Morton said. 'He's just crazy enough to start killing if he gets scared or wounded. We'd better get things straightened up around here Sergeant Crowther!'

Morton issued instructions for the road to be closed and enquired about progress on bringing Mark Roper, Bruno Costi and a priest to the scene. Sergeant Crowther told him that everything was done that could be done. I could see Morton's eyes drifting over the physiques of the dozen or so cops as he requested shields, bullet-proof vests and more weapons to be brought up.

Sergeant Crowther said, 'Should we call the heavy squad, sir?'

Morton looked at him. 'Do you think I'm an idiot, Sergeant?'

'No, sir.'

'You're right, I'm not. I'd rather try it myself

207

than let those bloody cowboys loose. It's brains that'll get us out of this, Sergeant.'

'Yes, sir.'

I'd been hanging around, listening, and keeping an eye on Ted Withers. A paramedic had arrived and said the wound was clean. The marksman asked him about the calibre of the bullet and the medic just stared at him. We were all operating on different wavelengths and I wondered how long Morton could hold it all together. He was doing a pretty good job, so far.

'Hardy,' he said, 'you look as if you're thinking. If you've got any bright ideas you might let me know.'

I shook my head. 'I was working out something about the Costis. I think I've got it, not that it's any help. Why's the father at home?'

I asked to try to get a line on how Morton felt about Sergei Costi. Whether he regarded him like Ted Withers, as expendable. But he just grunted which told me nothing, 'Semi-retired. Not too well.'

'I've got a number I was given by an Italian down south in the same line of business as Costi. He's the one whose daughter went missing. He said he had influence up here. He might have some ideas . . . '

'If you're thinking you can get him here to talk to Ronny the way you promised, forget it. This'll all be over long before that.'

'No,' I said, 'I'm just grasping at straws, like you.'

He shot me an evil look. 'Go with Sergeant Dexter. He's dropping in on the neighbours to tell them to keep their heads down. One of them'll let you use the phone if you ask nicely.'

He was dismissing me from the scene of action and we both knew it. There was no point in resisting; I wasn't going to personally attack the house with my 38 in my fist and a handkerchief wrapped around my head. It was a waiting game and we both knew it.

'He's tense,' the marksman said. 'Give me another three inches, mate. C'mon, two inches!'

I heard Morton say 'Wait,' again as I went off to find Sergeant Dexter.

The Sergeant wasn't happy with his assignment. He was a big-bellied cop, youngish for his rank but on the way to looking older. He didn't like me for being a civilian but he liked to talk and it balanced out. As we walked along the track towards the first of the houses, he told me that we should rush the Costi place now.

'He might kill everyone if we do that,' I said.

'Wouldn't get them all. He will if we leave it much longer.'

'Know him, do you?'

'Ronny? Sure I know him. He's as crazy as they come. I mean right across the board—bikes, booze, dope and religion.'

'They're getting a priest,' I said.

Dexter kicked a stone with his highly polished boot. 'Ronny's crazy enough to shoot him.'

'D'you know Sergeant Withers?'

'Yeah. She's all right. She can't help having that bastard as her old man.'

We reached the first place, a mock French

209

farmhouse, all sand-blasted brick and narrow windows. There was a small vineyard and orchard near the house with a lot of watering equipment. A four-wheel-drive stood outside. The owners, a nervous looking elderly couple wearing tailored overalls, stood on the front porch watching us as we approached.

'The police at last. Thank god,' the man said. 'Can you please tell us what's going on up there?' He inclined his old, bald head in the direction of the Costi house.

Dexter told him, with a minimum of detail, and advised him and his wife to keep inside. He also said that some men might have to come through their property.

'I don't know about that,' the woman said. 'We've got some very delicate plants in here.'

'We've got a wounded officer in the house,' Dexter said, 'and three other people in danger.'

'Italians. Dreadful people,' the woman said, 'They shouldn't be allowed . . . '

'Where's the phone?' I snapped.

The man pointed and I went down the hall past the bowls of flowers on stands and the framed family pictures. I grabbed the phone and dug out the card with Fanfani's number on it. Fanfani himself answered. I gave him a sketch of the situation, with the very briefest indication that Schmidt/Bach had committed more crimes than anyone had thought, and asked him if he had any ideas.

'The priest . . . '

'He's on his way.'

'I don't know these people. Where are they from?'

'I haven't a clue, Mr Fanfani. I just thought you might have something useful to contribute.'

'No. I could get a helicopter and . . . '

'It'll be finished by then. And I don't think you're going to be able to talk to the man who killed Werner Schmidt.'

'You mean the police will kill him?'

'No, Mr Fanfani. I don't mean that at all.' I rang off and hurried back to the front of the house. The old couple were still standing on the porch, looking up the hill towards the Costi house. I pushed past them.

'Aren't you going to pay for the call?' the man whined.

'No,' I said, 'and it was long distance, too.'

Dexter was out of sight when I got back to the road. I realised suddenly that I was tired and drained of physical and emotional energy. I sucked in deep breaths of the clean, country air and tried to pump myself up. I even pulled out the Smith & Wesson and checked its action. I did not feel better. I had a vision of Glen Withers lying on a white shagpile carpet with blood oozing from her and the young man I'd seen in the photograph at Mark Roper's house—the dark, snake-like man with the hooded eyes— standing over her with a rifle. My city shoes were stirring up the dust. I coughed and felt useless as I trudged back up to where all the other useless men with guns were. I knew I'd solved a problem but the solution was about as useful as a condom to a eunuch.

23

Back at the siege the cast of characters had expanded. There were two ambulances and several more police cars. Uniformed cops were holding the press people back behind yellow plastic tapes at either end of the road. Tension was hanging like dust in the air. Everyone who could take his frustration out on someone else was doing it. Morton used me. 'We can't find Roper,' he fumed, 'and the priest's at some old fart's funeral.'

'Why don't you round up a couple of Ronny's bikie mates? Could be useful.'

Morton stared at me. 'Bikies? Are you serious? With all this shit going on you want to bring in bikies?'

I shrugged. 'Just a suggestion. What does the sharpshooter say?'

'He says he's getting tired. I'm going to have to send someone in. We've got a volunteer.'

He pointed to where a tall, thin constable was changing into a blue overall, not unlike the one worn by Mark Roper. The bullet-proof vest he was wearing would make him look less thin and he didn't look a lot like Roper anyway. I wondered what they were going to put on his head.

'Commissioner.' The policeman who knew how radios worked was beckoning urgently. Morton went across and I followed. It was only a matter of time before he told me to piss off.

'He's got a CB,' the policeman said. 'He's sending. I can pick him up.'

'Do it!'

A bit of the code name rigmarole was gone through and then Renato Costi's voice, higher-pitched than before, came through. 'I told you I wanted Roper.'

'He's coming,' Morton said. 'Let me talk to someone else in the house.'

'No.'

'Are they all still alive?'

'Yes. For now they are.'

'Can't you let your mother and sister go at least?' I had to admire Morton; his voice was steady and he was trying to win a few points.

Ronny's voice went into a near shriek. 'Fuck you. What sister? Send Roper. That's all, cunt.'

Morton spoke quickly. 'There's a priest coming. He wants . . . '

'Fuck what he wants. You'll need him afterwards. That's it!'

The line went dead. Morton shook his head. 'Mad as a cut snake.'

He went over to the marksman who listened, nodded and fell into a relaxed posture. Then Morton went back to where the tall, thin, dark young policeman was standing. He had his

213

hands in the deep side pockets of the overall and I could see the bulge of his pistol in his right hand. Morton spoke to him, patted him on the shoulder. The young cop grinned and pushed back his hair which was long for a cop but not nearly as long as Roper's. I wanted to tell him to let it fall forward, but I didn't have the right to tell him anything. He conferred with the marksman and then began to walk towards a point where he would leave the shelter of the trees. The sharpshooter tucked the rifle butt into his shoulder. The breeze that had been stirring the leaves dropped. I stared at the top floor window; then I glanced around. I was holding my breath and everybody else was doing the same.

Before the man in the overall could break cover another figure appeared to his left, moving unsteadily but quickly forward. He stepped out of the shade into the sunlight. He was wearing a shirt and trousers. His right arm was strapped to his body and he held a pistol in his left hand.

'Ted.' Morton's voice was a harsh whisper. 'It's Ted Withers.'

The two shots came within a split second of each other. Withers' left arm went up and the gun flew from his hand as he staggered backwards and fell.

The marksman said, 'Got him!' A long, drawn-out scream came from the house.

The paramedic rushed forward and bent over

Withers. The face he turned towards us as we approached was ashen. 'I was looking at the house,' he said. 'I'm sorry. I'm sorry.'

Morton said, 'Is he dead?'

The medic nodded. 'Through the heart.'

Morton started barking instructions and suddenly the space in front of the house which had been still and empty was full of people and equipment. Two uniformed cops got to the front door first, closely followed by a pair of ambulance men with a stretcher. I stayed close to Morton. We went into the cool interior, a tiled hallway, and up the wide, curving staircase. We met the stretcher bearers coming down. Glen Withers' eyes were fluttering. She managed a weak grin as she recognised me.

'I'm okay,' she murmured. 'She told him—Mario.'

'I know,' I said. 'Don't worry.'

I glanced at one of the stretcher men who nodded.

'Leg,' he said. 'She's okay, but please . . . '

I touched Glen's shoulder as they whisked her past. From below I could hear women sobbing and soothing voices. Morton and I went up the stairs and along a carpeted corridor to a big front room. A constable standing guard stepped aside. Renato Costi, dressed in motor cycle boots, black jeans and navy singlet, lay on his back a few metres away from the shattered window. Blood and brain tissue had sprayed over the floor and walls. A rifle with a telescopic sight lay below the window and there must have been more than twenty cigarette butts ground out in the deep, pale pink carpet.

Morton crouched beside the body. 'An inch above the eye,' he said. 'That boy can really shoot.'

'So could Ronny,' I grunted.

'Ted was a sitting duck.'

Something about the way he said it, biting down on the words as if to cut them off, and the glance he shot at the constable, told me more than the statement itself. Had Ted Withers charged the house to rescue his daughter, provide the diversion for the sharpshooter to take advantage of, or to push Renato into taking care of Sergei Costi? Or to do the job himself? There was no doubt about the way it would appear in the record.

'He was a hero,' I said.

'Yup. Medals all round. Well, there's a lot of tidying up to do around here.' He straightened and walked to the door. 'Come on, Hardy. You shouldn't even be here. Constable, no-one except the technical people and the pathologist in this room, got it?'

'Yes, sir. The mother and father?'

'You heard me, son.'

Despite what he'd just said, Morton let me accompany him while he checked on the situation in the house. We learned that Renato had locked his father and mother in the wine cellar in the basement of the house. He had tied his sister to a chair in the room where Glen Withers had been shot. The girl had been in a faint or hysterical for most of the time. But she had heard the final shots and it was her scream that

216

had signalled the end of the business. She was now in the hands of a policewoman and the ambulance men. Morton conducted a brief interview with Sergei Costi from which I was excluded. Mrs Costi was in a state of collapse.

Bruno Costi, a stressed, balding man in his thirties, and a plump, avuncular priest arrived and were ushered inside the house to offer what comfort they could. A few other people turned up—all Italians, all distressed. A constable who spoke the language talked to them and allowed some in and turned others away. Two camera crews did some filming and reporters talked to a couple of cops. But Morton didn't come out and the reporter who tried to talk to me went away very unhappy.

When Barrett Breen arrived I angered the other newshounds by beckoning him over and going into a huddle with him. I gave him a scaled-down version of what I knew. Good stuff, but not the whole story. I needed to be on side with the police as much as I needed friends in the media. But Breen was satisfied; he scribbled notes, checked on name spellings and thanked me for honouring our agreement. The people with the microphones and cameras clustered around him after he left me but I didn't bother to watch. What he did with the information I'd given him was his business.

The police eventually shooed them back to the road. I sat on a piece of sandstone which was part of the artful, restrained landscaping of the front garden, and waited for Morton. There was a lot of coming and going, a lot of sweating and swearing as the afternoon grew warmer. A cop carried away Renato's rifle enclosed in a plastic bag, and Glen Withers' pistol, similarly wrapped. Then came Renato himself, all zipped up in a black vinyl body bag. Good stuff for the cameramen. There was still no sign of Morton so I wandered around the front of the house and looked at the two cars parked carelessly on the gravel together with Ronny's bike—a black and silver Kawasaki 1500 with raked handlebars, stripped to the chromium-plated bone. A death machine.

Morton emerged from the house wiping his face with a soggy handkerchief. He'd worn his jacket and tightly knotted tie throughout the whole business, but now he looked ready to strip down to his singlet and jockey shorts. He waved me over and I went, carrying my jacket slung over my shoulder. This allowed me to show off my gun in its holster which was the only thing that had stopped some of the cops telling me to piss off.

'Now I've got to talk to the press,' Morton said.

'It's tough at the top.'

'Fuck you. What did you do that counted?'

'I gave Ted Withers another hour or so of life. And if it hadn't been for him you'd still be sitting there with your finger up your arse.'

'I can see why not everyone in Sydney likes you.'

I sighed and suddenly felt old and empty. I wanted something to eat and drink and some-

218

one to be nice to me, and someone to be nice to. 'I've got a knack for getting into situations that bring out the worst in people, including me. What's next, Commissioner?'

'I hear you didn't want to get your face on television?'

'Right. They never get me on my best side.'

'Keep it that way. How do you stand with your clients?'

'Lousy,' I said.

Morton sucked in air and put the braided cap he'd been carrying back on his head. 'I'm going to talk bullshit for a few minutes. You go back to your motel and wait. We'll have a de-briefing at the hospital when Sergeant Withers is up to it.'

'When's that likely to be?'

Morton straightened his jacket. 'Tomorrow, I hope. Depends on how the news of her father's death affects her.'

24

One hospital is pretty much like another in my experience. They all use the same disinfectant and have the same bugs in the air conditioning. The Newcastle Community Hospital wasn't worse or better than average, but slightly more interesting in that it showed some signs of renovation and repair after earthquake damage. Twenty-four hours after the Costi siege Morton, a Chief Inspector named Reynolds and an Italian-speaking Sergeant who was the police ethnic community liaison officer, and I gathered at the bed of Senior Sergeant Glenys Withers.

After a nurse had told us what not to do, we took chairs around the bed. I sat a discreet distance from the patient. She looked good; her hair was brushed and shining and the little bit of weight she'd lost around the face suited her. The white hospital smock didn't do much for her though, nor the drip feed into her arm. We exchanged smiles while Morton and Reynolds made commiserating noises to Glen about her dad and then approving noises about her and each other. When Glen indicated that she was quite fit enough to talk, Morton invited a stenographer in and we got down to business.

Glen told us that she had set her radio to broadcast the alert signal if she didn't return within an hour.

'Sensible precaution,' Reynolds said. 'Sound procedure.'

Once inside the house she had requested a private talk with Gina Costi to which the girl had reluctantly agreed. 'She was terrified,' Glen said. 'Quite literally. She's not very bright and you could see she'd been under a lot of strain.'

'How did you handle it?' Morton said.

'I tried to be discreet. I said we'd received certain information about Oscar Bach and would she like to comment on her relations with him.'

'Who was in the house then?' I asked.

'I'd only seen Gina, Mr and Mrs Costi and the . . . servant, whatever she is.'

'Housekeeper,' the liaison man said. 'Mrs Adamo.'

Glen nodded. 'At first Gina didn't want to say anything. I pressed her a little, mentioned Mark Roper. Then it all came pouring out—how Bach had forced her to have sex with him, how Roper had done nothing, how she'd tried to keep quiet about it. She was ashamed, but more frightened than ashamed.'

'Frightened of what?' Morton said.

'Of her brother, of Renato. Apparently he's completely crazy about the idea of family honour. He's all hung up on old Italian ideas about virginity and dishonour and vendettas and all that. She's brainless, but she was sensible enough to be scared that Renato would kill her and Roper and Bach if he got the chance. She said he likes killing.'

I glanced at the liaison man's notepad. He was writing in Italian, underlining the words and adding exclamation marks. I had the rogue thought that Helen Broadway would have been able to translate his notes for me.

'Gina got drunk at Christmas last year. The strain of keeping it all in was too much for her and she told her brother Mario. She loves Mario. She says he's the gentlest of her brothers.'

'Not hard to edge out Ronny,' I said.

Morton signalled for me to shut up. 'Go on, Sergeant, if you feel up to it.'

'I'm all right, sir.'

She went on to spell out the chain of events as Gina understood them. This was pretty much how I'd worked it out in my own head, much too late for it to be of any use. Mario had told his father that he intended to kill Oscar Bach. For all his mildness, Mario was just as keen on honour as Renato, just more cunning about it. Mario had seized his opportunity in the chaos following the earthquake. He'd been keeping tabs on Bach, come on him just as he'd avoided being injured when the church collapsed and had attacked him with a brick. The trouble was, Bach had fought. Mario had killed him and done enough to make it look as if Bach was a quake victim, but he'd been badly injured in the fight himself and ended up comatose in hospital.

'This was what Gina and her father pieced together,' Glen said. 'Mario had told Sergei Costi all about it and how he planned to kill Bach.'

'Mario must have really done some work on Bach,' I said. 'Somehow he found out that he was Werner Schmidt. Was Mario a drinker?'

'Gina says he was,' Glen said.

'He phoned up Antonio Fanfani when he was drunk. That was just before opportunity knocked on December 28. That explains why Sergei ordered the work to be done on the Ocean Street place. He was hoping to clean away anything that Bach might have left lying around.'

Reynolds consulted a file. 'Mr Costi wanted to demolish the building, but he was prevented by a regulation requiring buildings over a certain age to be inspected for possible heritage value.'

'Sergeant,' Morton said.

Glen was beginning to look tired, but she took a drink of water and went on. 'Renato was in the house. He listened to all this. He must've because ... after, I heard him shouting and raving and parroting Gina's exact words back at her. He must've locked his mother and father and the housekeeper away somewhere. Then he burst in on Gina and me. He was completely crazy. We fought over my weapon, but he got it and ... he shot me. I heard things after that, but I was in shock and none of it makes much sense until I saw Cliff on the stairs.'

'Mr Hardy has been of considerable use,' Morton said smoothly.

'Did they find bodies at the house?' Glen said.

Morton nodded. 'Two.'

Then I remembered that the only person I'd told about Bach's interest in the lagoon was Ted Withers and he was dead. It wasn't the time to make the point. Morton asked a few more questions and invited Reynolds and the liaison man to do the same. There was nothing more of substance to add. He thanked Glen and wished her a speedy recovery.

'I'd like a to have a word with Cliff, please,' Glen said.

Morton put his braided cap on. 'Certainly. I'd like to see you, too, Mr Hardy. In ten minutes, shall we say?'

They trooped out and I went to the bed and kissed Glen s now slightly damp forehead. Then I took her hand and played with it, the way you do. 'I'm sorry about your father,' I said. 'He gave it a very good try.'

Her eyes were wet. She sniffed and shook her head. 'He was corrupt. He knew that I knew. It was very difficult. Only a matter of time. I'm glad he didn't finish up inside or on the front seat of his car with a shotgun. You know.'

'Sure,' I said.

'What does Morton want with you now?'

'I don't know. If he wants to get nasty I'll say I won't tell him where the other bodies are.'

Her eyes widened. 'Where are they?'

224

'I think they're in the Redhead lagoon.'

'Jesus. I think I want to get out of this place. If I'm fit I might apply for a transfer to Sydney.'

'That's a good idea,' I said.

Assistant Commissioner Morton wanted to debrief me the way he had Glen. I wasn't too co-operative, but I did tell him about the lagoon.

He shook his head. 'Weird world isn't it? You come up here looking for a killer and you find him. You know where Mario Costi is, don't you?'

'No.'

'He's about two floors above.'

'What'll happen there?'

'Nothing. He's not improving, close to brain dead. They'll be pulling the plug pretty soon.'

I didn't envy the cops what they had to do next—dragging ponds, identifying bodies and informing relatives is not fun, but I didn't imagine much of that would fall to Morton's lot. He had something else on his mind.

'Did you get much of a chance to talk to Ted Withers before he went over the top, Hardy?'

'Not much. Why?'

'I just wondered about his state of mind.'

I didn't say anything and we walked down the hospital corridor to the elevator. Reynolds and the stenographer had gone and we had the lift to ourselves. 'I'm in a position to do Glenys Withers a bit of good,' Morton said.

'I imagine you are.'

'Or not, as the case may be.'

I nodded. We reached the ground floor and Morton reached for my hand again, the way he had the day before. It was an odd gesture for such a restrained man. 'There are some ladies and gentlemen from the press wanting to talk to you. Watch what you say, won't you?'

I did better than that. I jumped back into the lift, went up a few floors to where I could get across to another wing, and left the building through a side entrance. After the siege, the cops had taken me back to my motel. I'd caught a cab to the hospital; now I caught another one to where my car was parked near the police building with an infringement notice flapping in the breeze under the windscreen wiper. I wondered whether Morton was in a position to fix it for me.

I drove to Dudley and pulled up outside the Jacobs' house in Bombala Street. There was a red BMW parked outside. May Jacobs met me at the door with a smile and a kiss.

'Ralph's here,' she whispered. 'He's having a good talk with his father. The first in years. They're going to the football today.'

'That's nice,' I said.

'I want to thank you. It was an awful business. Those poor people.'

There had been some rather garbled coverage of the activity in Dudley and Kahiba in the press, but May would have picked up some more solid dope from the locals. I heard a laugh coming from further inside the house. May smiled.

'I just came to explain a few things to Horrie or try to,' I said. 'I don't know how he feels about Oscar Bach now but . . . '

'We talked last night. He said Oscar must have had a split personality—crazy and not crazy. Even a man who did such awful things needs a friend.'

It seemed as good a way as any to leave it. Bach may have been cultivating Horrie to get at his money or his granddaughters. We'd never know. 'Yeah,' I said, 'that's about it.'

'I want to pay you, Cliff.'

'Horrie already paid me. I'll be going, May. Give them both my regards.'

She kissed me again. 'Ralph says you beat him in a fight.'

I grinned and the healed cuts on my face hurt a little. I also felt some pain in the knee Wrecker had worked on. 'It was a draw,' I said.

I was halfway back to Sydney, heading in the other direction, before I remembered Helen Broadway's phone message: 'Give me a call, hey?' Well, maybe I would, but then again, maybe not. For a man in my game there's something very attractive about a policewoman who knows the score and has a house on the coast.